BEST OF THE

Winning and Shortlisted Stories

2023-2024

Edited by Ed Bicioc & Amanda Scotland

NOT QUITE WRITE PRESS

First published in 2024 by Not Quite Write Press

Not Quite Write Press
ABN 85 157 104 734
PO Box 9067
Wyoming NSW 2250
Australia
notquitewrite.com

A catalogue record for this book is available from the National Library of Australia

Best of the Not Quite Write Prize for Flash Fiction 2023-2024: Winning and Shortlisted Stories

ISBN 978-1-7637165-0-6 (paperback)
ISBN 978-1-7637165-1-3 (eBook)

Edited by Ed Bicioc and Amanda Scotland (non-Australian English spellings retained)
Internal design by Amanda Scotland
Cover illustration and design by Vanessa Browne, Vee Creative

Write on!

— Ed & Amanda

CONTENTS

FOREWORD...**ix**

INTRODUCTION ....**xiii**

   About the Not Quite Write Prize xiii
   WTF is an anti-prompt?... xvi
   About the judges xvii

2023   **19**

   OVERVIEW **20**

      THE INTERROGATION...**21**
         Remy Joll

      I CARRIED YOU **27**
         Gwendaline Higgins

      BACHMEIER BRIDGE, SUMMER '08.................**33**
         Em Arata-Berkel

      MODERN HUMAN..**39**
         Charles Byrne

      TRULY, MADLY, DEEPLY **45**
         Kathy Prokhovnik

      UNTITLED #2 ....**51**
         Greg Schmidt

   2023 LONGLIST...**58**

JANUARY 2024   **61**

    OVERVIEW.. 62

        IT NEVER RAINS BUT IT POURS 63
        Athena Law

        BLESS THIS MESS.. 69
        Chad Frame

        AS FAR AS THE EYE CAN SEE.. 75
        Tess Allen

        A FUNNY STORY 81
        Dean Koorey

        THE WAY OF THE BINS... 88
        Bob Topping

        THE EARLY BIRD CATCHES THE WORM 94
        Anne Wilkins

    JANUARY 2024 LONGLIST 100

APRIL 2024   **103**

    OVERVIEW.. 104

        UNSAY ANYTHING 105
        Chad Frame

        EVERYONE'S A WINNER.. 112
        Sam James

        A GUIDE TO JUDGING THE PIE ENTRIES AT THE WOMEN'S AUXILIARY CLUB ANNUAL FAIR.............. 118
        Sally Simon

        HOT GIRL SUMMER 125
        Laura J. Rayne

        ADVENTURE AWAITS.. 130
        Terra Babcock

        SURVIVAL GUIDE TO STAYING SINGLE 136
        M. Lea Gray

    APRIL 2024 LONGLIST 142

JULY 2024   **145**

    OVERVIEW **146**

        TWELVE JARS **147**
        Autumn Bettinger

        IT'S HEADING FOR EARTH AND SPOILER ALERT: WE DON'T STAND A CHANCE **153**
        Dean Koorey

        BLURPLE **160**
        Roxanne Kubiak

        PENNVILLE PARK **165**
        George Faville

        OFF ROAD **172**
        R. C. Barajas

        THE EASTER BUNNY IS COMING! **178**
        Tabbie Hunt

    JULY 2024 LONGLIST **185**

OCTOBER 2024   **189**

    OVERVIEW **190**

        I TOLD YOU THIS WAS A POEM **191**
        Taurenelle

        NINE TIMES SEVEN IS SIXTY-THREE **198**
        Emily Rinkema

        THE TIP OF THE TONGUE THE TEETH THE LIPS **203**
        Eilish Forwells

        LOVE STRUCK BY A LAMPPOST **209**
        J. Lewis-Edney

        SHARPENED STAKES **216**
        Sheridan Bell

        RIDE IT TO HEAVEN **223**
        W. J. Arthur

    OCTOBER 2024 LONGLIST **229**

Foreword

Two and a half years ago, Amanda had the brilliant idea to start a podcast.

It was a Friday evening, and we were several glasses of merlot deep into a *Furious Fiction* brainstorming session. We had mind-mapped each of the prompts, developed lists of potential genres, themes, characters and plot points, and elaborated on a few of the most promising ones. Our hope was to elicit that mysterious flash of inspiration that drives writers to obsessively bash away at the keys until the finished product is exorcised from the depths of their souls.

By the end of the evening, my laptop screen was brimming with ideas, but precious few completed sentences or actual, countable words. But what had stood out was the conversation, which had digressed often from the topic at hand to the wider aspects of writing – which elements of story were most important, which rules to abide by and which to ignore, and how we would do things differently if we were to run our own flash fiction competition. We talked about other things, too, like the news, pop culture, and what movies and TV shows we had been watching. Weaving these broader elements of life and culture into the conversation felt natural, and perhaps somehow necessary to the creative process, and this became the template for what would become the *Not Quite Write Podcast*.

The feeling of uploading the first episode of a new podcast is similar to hitting the submit button for a flash fiction competition. Both are met with a resounding and protracted silence, which affords you plenty of time to dwell on all your greatest fears and insecurities. In a way, we were comforted in those early days by the fact that nobody was listening. But we kept talking, and soon enough, more and more of you did start to tune in.

It's been incredible to see *Not Quite Write* come so far, so quickly, from such tentative beginnings. Thanks to the podcast, we've had the honour of interviewing dozens of accomplished authors at the *Words on the Waves* writers' festival. The *Not Quite Write Prize* has allowed us to indulge our fantasy of hosting our own writing competition. And today, this anthology marks the launch of *Not Quite Write Press* and opens the newest chapter of our story. Though this journey has felt so unexpected, it's fitting that a friendship which began twenty years ago at a small printing company should eventually deliver a printed book.

When we began the *Not Quite Write Prize*, we wanted to imbue it with the same playful spirit with which we approach the podcast. Writing is both a craft to be studied and a form of individual artistic expression. Like all great works of art, the best stories combine technical proficiency with a willingness to bend the rules towards the artist's vision. We believe that it is necessary to study the technical elements of writing, but it is equally important to find that vehicle for your own personal expression, and to write for the absolute joy of it.

We have been thrilled to see these sentiments embraced by the community of writers who have shared their work with us, and we are proud to present this anthology to showcase the very best stories from the first five rounds of the competition.

These are stories that explore the spectrum of human experience. They have touched our hearts, sent chills down our spines, and on more than one occasion have caused us to nearly soil ourselves with laughter (perhaps at the behest of a mysterious Scotsman). These stories should not be read aloud in polite company.

Many of our shortlisters are already accomplished authors and recipients of accolades far more impressive than ours. Their talent and creativity have challenged our own tastes and assumptions. We had at one time advised entrants to avoid submitting poetry, and yet poems have shortlisted in the *Not Quite Write Prize* on more than one occasion.

Alongside the stories you will find additional background and insights from their authors as well as our commentary. Aside from enjoying the stories themselves, we hope this collection will serve as a sort of 'how-to' for writers looking for inspiration and wishing to hone their own craft.

We would like to extend a huge congratulations to all our winning and shortlisted stories for 2023 and 2024, and a massive thank you to each and every person who has entered the *Not Quite Write Prize*. We are overwhelmed by the response this competition has had in the community, and we are honoured that you have chosen to share your work with us.

Please enjoy what we hope will be the first of many anthologies to come.

— Ed

Introduction

About the Not Quite Write Prize

We first set out to create the *Not Quite Write Prize* with the goal of drawing listeners to the *Not Quite Write Podcast*. Little did we know it would soon come to consume our every waking moment, much like that intense summer fling who turns up unexpectedly at your high school with pompoms in hand and a glint in her eye, promising to grease your lightning.

And we wouldn't have it any other way.

The inaugural competition, held in July 2023, was free to enter and offered a modest first prize of AU$300 for stories up to 600 words based on two prompts and one anti-prompt. The prize money fluttered from our own wallets like so many moths, but we saw it as a small price to pay to connect with more like-minded people. *Surely*, we thought, *we can't be the only ones who would find our jokes funny, and our banter endearing?*

We designed the original *Not Quite Write Prize* to run in a similar format to the Australian Writers' Centre's *Furious Fiction*, into which we were occasional entrants at the time. The 600-word count was our feeble attempt to differentiate ourselves from *Furious Fiction*, however it was the anti-prompt and podcast commentary which would become the *Not Quite Write Prize's* key points of difference.

With our limited reach and knowing how busy writers are, we thought we'd be lucky to get 20 entrants to that first round. We were knocked sideways when we received nearly 700 entries!

Faced with that tsunami of enthusiasm, we nevertheless both committed to reading every single story. The winner of that round remains our most hotly contested argument to date (with me winning the argument on that occasion and, let's face it, most occasions since – that expensive law degree has to prove its worth somehow.)

We had so much fun running the first competition that it was an easy decision to keep going. We reasoned that the only sustainable way to continue was to charge an entry fee, but also that this would allow us to offer more and greater prizes and participant features. We brought the word count back down to 500 to manage our reading time but kept all other aspects of the competition the same. We also began offering written feedback plus our beloved on-air 'Daredevil' critiques, which have become a hallmark of the competition. Who knew writers were such masochists?

That first paid round of the competition was nerve-racking. Would writers still want to compete if they had to pay for the privilege? Indeed some writers were not happy with this turn of events. The hate mail we received has to be among the most eloquent hate mail ever written.

Still, we knew we had something special, and we were determined to make it a long-term success. We risked a much higher cash prize offering for 2024 and worked our butts off to set up the website infrastructure and get the word out.

Validating our faith in the comp and ourselves, we received an astonishing 257 entries in January 2024. Since then, we've managed to keep our entry numbers consistent with far less legwork, leaving us time to focus on continuously improving the competition and on creating new and exciting things – like the anthology you now hold in your hands!

It's our dream to take *Not Quite Write* full-time and give both the podcast and the competition the commitment they deserve. We remain immensely grateful to every person who has helped to spread the word about our little corner of the internet.

We can't wait to see what 2025 and beyond holds for us all.

— Amanda

WTF is an anti-prompt?

Like many writing competitions, the *Not Quite Write Prize* uses creative writing prompts to inspire and challenge entrants. Unlike other competitions, it also includes something called an *anti-prompt*. The anti-prompt challenges entrants to break a traditionally accepted 'rule' of writing while still telling a great story.

The art of writing is a no-holds-barred creative pursuit which will look different for everyone. The craft of writing, however, is subject to many helpful precepts which can guide writers to elevate their prose. These are what we call the writing 'rules'. Understanding these rules can help writers craft more compelling stories.

When we ask entrants to break a writing rule, we're not issuing a license to ignore the rule and its reason for existing. Instead, we're challenging them to think about why the rule exists, to recognise how it works to elevate prose, and then find a creative way to break the rule without breaking their story.

In this anthology, you will observe some of the many creative ways our authors have approached the following anti-prompts:

Break the rule 'avoid all adverbs' (July 2023)
Break the rule 'avoid clichés' (January 2024)
Break the rule 'always use said' (April 2024)
Break the rule 'avoid purple prose' (July 2024)
Break the rule 'avoid head-hopping' (October 2024)

About the judges

Ed

Ever since he placed second in a high school short story competition, Ed has fancied himself as something of a writer.

He is a self-confessed literary masochist, whose disdain of happy endings and preference for arduous and harrowing literature have earned him the title, 'Case-hardened Wowser.'

Aside from being a serial writing-competition entrant, his hobbies include avoiding Vegemite, abhorring ellipses, and obsessively rewriting opening sentences.

Amanda

Amanda was first published in *The Sydney Morning Herald* at the tender age of seven with a charming poem about the joy of Christmas.

Since then, Amanda has gone on to enjoy wider publication, including opinion pieces and feature articles across major Australian mastheads and industry magazines, as well as the occasional flash and micro zine.

Amanda's competitive spirit extends from the page to the small screen, having won prizes for both her fiction (thanks *Furious Fiction!*) and her quiz show prowess.

Amanda identifies as a 'plotter' and sprinkles commas like salt. She is currently editing her middle-grade novel, set in an abandoned theme park. Will her novel ever see the light of day? Time will tell...

2023

Overview

The inaugural *Not Quite Write Prize for Flash Fiction* in 2023 challenged writers to create an original piece of fiction of no more than 600 words, which:

included the word **RITE**.

included the action **'crossing a line'**.

broke the writing rule **'avoid all adverbs'**.

The competition drew **678** entries from authors in **51** countries around the world. That's **406,800** words for our judges, Ed and Amanda, to read. That's about the same number of words as ***Don Quixote*** **by Miguel de Cervantes**.

Please enjoy the following top six stories from this round of the competition...

THE INTERROGATION

Remy Joll

'Did you really do that?' she asks.

Neither denying it nor fessing up seems like a good option. 'Possibly,' I say.

She frowns. 'Did you know what you were doing?'

I honestly don't know the answer. 'Vaguely.'

'Did you think it through?'

There was no thinking on my part. There was the smell of cookies escaping the oven and the rain pounding so hard on the windows that it blocked off the rest of the world. And then there was us both laughing at the dough that had gotten in her hair, and me, trying to get it out, leaning in close and discovering that her hair had a smell of its own. 'Regrettably, no,' I say.

She raises her chin, signaling that the toughest questions are yet to come. 'Are you aware that there's a line?'

I suppose I've been dimly aware of the line, but it's only now that it's shown itself. It has, in fact, taken control of the universe. 'Keenly aware,' I say.

I don't know how she knew it was a kiss. My lips barely touched her hair. My face must have lingered. She pulled away with an alarming look, then turned and commanded me to follow. I complied and marched to the sitting room, where she directed me to the sofa. She pulled her chair up close, as if I were a flight risk.

She continues. 'Do you know where the line is? Can you see it clearly?'

Her eyes are intense. I drop my gaze to her legs, just inches from mine. She wears a skirt that reaches just above her knees. It's blue, the skirt, and a thin strip of orange runs along the hem, showing off both the blue and the tone of her skin. 'Stunningly clearly,' I say.

She absently runs her fingers back and forth along the bottom of her skirt, pulling it taut across her knees. 'And you know it's a line that perhaps, in theory, is crossable, but that once traversed, might be impossible to cross back over?'

I haven't given this a moment of thought until now, of course, but I'm catching up quickly. 'Miserably aware, yes.'

What does she usually wear? Jeans and t-shirts? Overalls? I have no idea. But I know exactly how the blue skirt clings to her hips, and how it falls against her calves when she's standing, and how, when she sits, it slides up and the hem traces a bright orange line across her knees.

She says, 'You've always been a true friend, right?'

This is not the sort of thing we usually ask each other, but I give it a go. I think through our history and the answer comes easily. 'Unfailingly,' I say.

She takes a deep breath. 'To me,' she says, 'among all the wonderful things in the world, some of which I have and some of which I only dream, a true friend is among the dearest, and this dear thing is to be put at risk only for something more beautiful still.' She pauses, then says, 'Do you see it like that?'

I want to say, 'assuredly, yes,' but I think she's had enough of my trite responses. I pull my eyes away from her legs and look at her eyes. I just nod.

Her face has softened. She seems to be out of questions, other than the big silent one—the one posed by the tears filling her eyes. This question turns out to be the easiest. I put my hands on her knees and lean across the orange line. Way across.

About the author

Remy Joll lives in Honolulu, Hawaii, and squeezes writing into days otherwise filled with ocean policy work, swimming, family, and friends.

Author's insights

'The prompt to include something about "crossing a line" got me thinking about boundaries in human relationships, and that led me to the theme of friends-to-lovers, which has plenty of room for suspense and the potential for both brutal and happy endings. I don't know why I chose the ending that I did. On another day, in a different mood, I might have gone with the other kind!'

Ed's comments

Our winner has crafted a multidimensional scene that invokes all the senses: the taste and smell of freshly baked cookies, the sound of rain on a window, the feeling of hair on the lips, and the tantalising sight of a thin orange hem on a blue skirt, which serves as a literal counterpart to the figurative 'line' that is the centrepiece of this story.

But it's really the story itself, with its powerful emotional core, that makes this a winner. It captures a real human moment, by bringing the characters to life and building tension towards a conclusion you genuinely care about. You can't help but get caught up in it.

Amanda's comments

This story was a standout for me from my very first read, and I didn't stop thinking about it throughout the judging process. The author addressed both the 'crossing the line' prompt and the 'avoid all adverbs' anti-prompt with flair. The choice to embed multiple adverbs in dialogue was a clever one, and it really fed the charm of the piece.

Still, what ultimately sold me was the story itself. I found myself becoming very invested in these characters and the outcome of this conversation. I was flooded with relief when our protagonist finally made their move. I must confess, I do love a happy ending (happy beginning?)

This story showcases the author's technical ability through an artful handling of the prompts. It offers a prime example of all the elements of plot, character and theme working together in harmony.

I CARRIED YOU

Gwendaline Higgins

You don't know what it means, but I carried you.

In the hopeful days and nights, the looking-forward weeks, the in-between time that stretched to over yonder, and stretched and stretched, until you.

I carried you, those sleepless nights, with the perfect weld of your too-new body outside against mine, through the fog-stunned times—the wistful times of sing-song whispers and that new knot longingly under my ribs, filling to breathlessness the place where I made you. Oh, how I carried you.

I carried you, the heedless days. Out of trees and friends' houses, up and out from tangles of bushes, bedclothes and fears, hauling the precarious roar and crash of your emotions, your sleepy abandon over expanses of country, bustling streets and dim-lit evenings. If you knew, the way the weight of you turned heavier in my arms and firmer on my hip, all the ways you became livelier over my shoulders and impatient off my lap.

I witnessed you. I caught the moments, the seconds that fleetingly mattered and that you could not see, catching them like the things that slid oblivious from your hands. I held the memories that would not hold, and I carried them too, I carried the mounting cargo of the memories of you as you walked and ran and wondered.

As you walked and ran and wondered ahead.

You carried me.

You carried me to the resting place, went along with those absurd rites they do.

You keep on carrying me, a sometimes-there weight in the stride of your legs, in your eyes that see the world and imagine much more, in your heart that I made. Until the looking-forward weeks have ended like a cliff, and you tumble into what it meant.

You know it now, don't you?

In the all-encompassing weld of the too-new body against yours, in the sudden narrowing of the world, in the heftier shadow of me in your world that goes on—the wondrous wisdom of how much you were loved.

I have been waiting for you to know it.

How longingly and forever-and-ever-after, how beyond-the-words it is that you were loved.

Oh, how, how I loved you.

They carry you to the resting place. They carry you carrying me. (Those rites are absurd, aren't they?) How weightless I am these days.

How tempting is the earth: the wondrous, wistful abandon of it. The earth upon which I, once, carried you... How tempting the driftings of the lines—

On the other side, will it be forgotten—just how much I loved you?

About the author

Gwendaline Higgins is French-Australian and lives and writes in two languages. Her fiction was shortlisted for the francophone Young Writer's Prize, *Prix du Jeune Ecrivain*. She currently resides in Paris.

Author's insights

'While the theme of this story will feel familiar and personal to many parents, it was at least in some part inspired — or perhaps triggered — by a short story by Alix E. Harrow, *A Whisper in the Weld* (*Shimmer* #22, November 2014). The *Not Quite Write Prize* helpfully provided the deadline and prompts to finish it off.'

Note: This story was resubmitted with edits for this anthology.

Ed's comments

This story really captures the anxiety and awe of parental love, the knowledge that it will never quite be reciprocated, and the enduring hope that your child may one day come to understand you through their own children.

It tells the story of our lives from a perspective I hadn't encountered before, and with language that is beautiful and evocative. It was an early frontrunner for me. I found it incredibly moving.

Amanda's comments

This author bravely ignored our advice to avoid poetry, delivering what might be described as a prose poem. This piece is full of beautiful metaphors that perfectly capture the beauty and pain of parenthood. I lost my dad while pregnant with my second child, so the emotional resonance for me was particularly strong.

I think a more subtle handling of the 'crossing the line' and 'rite' prompts would have elevated this piece, however I'm delighted to be proven wrong about the place of poetry in flash fiction competitions!

BACHMEIER BRIDGE, SUMMER '08

Em Arata-Berkel

Jumping off Bachmeier Bridge began with my grandparents, back when failing farms meant there was little else to do but take risks. Dad called it a family rite of passage, so the day after we rolled into his ancestral village, he took my brother Michael and me for a hike along county roads. By the time we reached the old suspension bridge, all three of us were sweatslick. That was supposed to motivate us, but standing up there in last year's swimsuit, my toes gripped the edge. My knees knocked.

Instead of the creek below, I studied broccoli treetops and counted my breaths the way Mom taught me. Dad said I'd be fine so long as I aimed right. I was supposed to fling myself toward the rocky bluff. Supposedly, the water next to it was deepest. The golden shallow end where the local girls applied sunscreen to each other's shoulders, that was dangerous. I could kill myself on that underwater shelf. Michael told me it'd crack my head like an egg. Dad said not to look at it, because looking at it could make me aim wrong.

The local girls were watching. They pointed toward the bluff, where Dad treaded water after his swan dive. They were all blonde and freckled. They looked like they could've been my cousins or maybe big sisters. I wanted to ask if they'd jump with all of us holding hands, but Dad hollered for me to hurry.

'Don't think about it,' he said, and I screamed when Michael shoved me.

He hooked me with the same arm then laughed as he jerked me back over the edge. My butt hit the bridge's wood. Girlish giggling bubbled up from below. My eyes stung.

'Remember what Dad said,' Michael chided. He offered his hand.

I blinked fast and muttered something about dust before taking it.

We'd ventured into the Ozarks to take a break from tears. Dad had pitched the road trip as spending summer vacation with family, but Michael told me we were just schmoozing for a place to stay. Everything we owned sat in the van parked outside Great Aunt Kathy's hunting lodge. That evening, we were supposed to meet her for dinner, bring our own Bachmeier Bridge stories, and let her weave them into the family mythology.

Michael pulled me to my feet, and while I crept toward the bridge's edge, he hung off the suspension wires. Leaning out over the water, he had his eyes on the bikini-clad sunbathers.

'I'm going to show Kat how it's done.'

Dad gave the okay, and Michael took a running start.

After he flung himself to gravity's whim, I couldn't see his face, but when I think back on it, I imagine he understood the stupid thing he'd done. I imagine his smile dropped and his features cycled through all the same feelings Dad's did when we got the call about Mom. At the end of it, I imagine there wasn't a single crease left on my brother's face.

That's how it was for Dad, and like Dad, my brother didn't scream.

Michael landed feet first with a wet crack. He hit the shelf, just a foot shy of safe, and once he'd collapsed, his legs floated at ragdoll angles. He bled beautifully. A muddy red boundary smeared between glinting shallows and the pond scum-colored water we were aiming for.

Sometimes I wonder if that made my jump easier, but like Dad said, I didn't actually think much about it. I saw my brother the way Mom appeared in nightmares, and I jumped after him.

About the author

Em Arata-Berkel enjoys creative writing, jumping into rivers, and other dubious activities. Their work appears in *I Sing The Salmon Home: Poems from Washington State*, *50 Word Stories*, and *101 Words*.

Author's insights

'Nestled in the Ozarks, there really is a tiny "German town" with a rusty old bridge kids used to jump from. My family took the plunge and immigrated there in pursuit of the American dream over a hundred years ago. Their descendants took their own plunges and sought fortunes in faraway cities — with mixed results. Today, my relatives still visit that initial landing pad to touch base and reconnect with what remains of their roots.'

Ed's comments

I loved the way this hinted at a much larger story but left the details to the reader's imagination. Failing farms, cracked eggs, stinging eyes: these are the details that build tension. The evocative language produces a disturbing undertone and a palpable sense of dread.

We never find out exactly what happened to the mother, but we do see how profoundly her death haunts her family. The ending is tragic, and I was left wondering whether this was simply a case of accidental misjudgement, or whether there was a hint of some darker intentionality in Michael's jump. I love the ambiguity.

Amanda's comments

I wasn't sure how I felt about this story on my first read; one thing I did know was that it had me hooked. This author offers us a masterclass in the artful development of backstory and tension.

It was perhaps the author's decision to leave much of the story lurking beneath the surface that kept me from connecting more deeply with the characters. Nevertheless, the story itself is a memorable one and continues to deliver with each read.

MODERN HUMAN

Charles Byrne

Listen, bro, I told you, I'm on all them apps – Hinge, Tinder, Bumbly, Bagel Dates. Shit, I even gots my OkCupid from the day! So many chatbots on that one I finna get me some honestly goodness genuine robot dates soon, lmfao. Like they do in Japan. For real, I saw them shits on BBC, they gots androidships there.

My point is what's a Harvard-educated lady in Manhattan with the cupid mouth of Clara Bow doing swiping right on me in the first place? It's GOTTA be some kind of fracking joke, amirite?

And you know I loves me some Harvard, prestige-wise. She don't even have to graduate, she could pull a Zuckerburger, I don't give three shits.

We could do up our little Paterson, NJ, house like two Blue Mountain knick-knacker motherfuckers. Shit, she could bring the bacon home from Manahatta and fry it up in a pan and I'd be the artist.

I know what you saying right now: you'd still be on them apps! Fuck yeah, bro! Cause she'd leave my ass in a heartbite! Even after I handymanned the house, painted the deck, installed those little metal hooks in her closet, and walked around all shirtless swoll like Terry Motherfucking Crew with all them little veins everywhere, with a toolbelt on. You know why? Because she sees me as a friend, bro!

I know this because text tells me so. Right now – this ain't some snapdat shit, text is forever, bro. And I'm tryna cipher that shit like it's the lawyer's paradox? 'Sees me'? 'As'? What does that literally mean? And what friend vibration did I emanate? Like instead of chumzoning me, she coulda said I dry her up like the Atacama, shit would at least be honest? Or she didn't feel the 'sparkler'. Or she is just downright lacking in the feeling of respect department for me as a human being. Or I deserve metooing. Like that shit would be messed up, but I'd understand it, you feel me?

My masculinity was compromised like a motherfucker, broheem. And by unseen forces.

We had went on three dates. I'm not an animal, you know that, my roll's slow, so I dry-pecked her cheek like a pigeon on the first date. Then on the second date right as her bus was pulling up I took her arm all gentle-like and asked her milady... and we had the sweetest, warmest kiss, broheem. It was like eating warm flapjacks straight off the griddle at Nana's, you know the feeling?

But then that third date. I heaved some vulnerable shit, like how I cried at that Sade concert, or how I like giving oral coitionals better than receiving it. Goddamn Hennessey. Funny, she liked saying vulnerable shit when it was her turn, all giggly, but when it was my turn, her face did this thing, it was like her eyes zoomed in a microsecond while the rest of her face zoomed back a microsecond.

Bro, it was like those job interviews where you are supposed to say how bad you are at shit, but it better not be something actually bad, or some song and jiggy we heard before, you piece of actual shit?

You see what happened next. A facefull of hair, then a mouth like a drawed-up drawbridge. Then the text a full day after my text.

Bro, tell me. Tell me how to be a modern huMan. Shit ain't working out for me. I'm an anachronism. Or catachronism.

You heard me!

I don't want an incelship.

Don't let them incel me, broheem!

About the author

Charles Byrne is a writer in the USA and erstwhile visitor to Australia with stories in American journals that include *Emrys*, *Gavialidae*, and *Scarlet Leaf Review*.

Author's insights

'Rather than share what inspired this story, I'd prefer to let the story speak for itself.'

Ed's comments

This kind of writing is deceptively difficult to pull off. Here, the author has created an entirely recognisable and compelling character from voice alone. And despite the surface-level lingo, our Modern Human is a surprisingly complex dude. He watches silent movies and the BBC. He affects an exterior of aloofness, but it's the juxtaposition between his masculinity and his sensitivity, romantic tendencies and consuming desire for domestic life that gives his character dimension, and indeed reflects something of what it is to be a man in the modern world.

Amanda's comments

Epic display of voice, *amirite?*

This is one of those stories that shone so bright in one area (in this case, voice), that I was able to overlook any potential shortcomings in other areas (like plot). While I would have loved more of a plot to latch onto, I still found myself completely invested in this unique huMan's plight.

I felt the author did an excellent job of capturing a young male perspective of the *Me Too* zeitgeist. It's clear the character's bravado masks deep fear and disappointment, and I couldn't help but be swept up in his heaved-up 'vulnerable shit'.

TRULY, MADLY, DEEPLY

Kathy Prokhovnik

If there is a fly in this rose-scented salve of a relationship, it is Harry. A small dog that, even after six months of acquaintance, bares his teeth at me when I pat him. I suppose he has some doggy seventh sense, or he just doesn't like sycophants. In my flat, but not at Samuel's place, Harry likes to sleep on the sofa and shit on the floor when left behind. Samuel says, 'Who's a naughty Harry boy then,' and rubs his woolly head.

It's a special sofa. I changed a lot of things in the flat when Philip died. I moved my bed into the small bedroom with a tree outside the window. I had the threadbare carpet replaced. I bought a new, very expensive sofa in a deep burnt orange, a lovely colour that Philip would have hated. When I bought it, it was an act of rigid, pointless rebellion, staring down Philip's ghost and raging against his carelessness in getting sick, and dying. Now it's the sofa where Samuel first put his hand on my knee, and moved it up my leg, and my back melted into the cushions.

The day that Samuel and I go shopping together we leave Harry in the flat with a special pig's ear treat that is meant to keep him happy. We catch the bus to the shops, and I find myself in the men's section on the eighth floor. It's some years since I've been in this foreign land. A sales assistant breezes across, pointing out corduroy trousers and merino wool scarves. Samuel laughs and says he's a moleskins and blue shirt person himself, takes one of the scarves and drapes it around my neck. 'Ahh,' he says. 'That is, wow.' He kisses my forehead.

I sit on a padded seat looking out a seventh-floor window, waiting for Samuel to emerge from the change room. Adele's earnest tones loop around us, pouring out of the ceiling or the walls, slightly too loud, slightly too distorted to move you. Poor Adele.

Who is this calm person, patient and smiling, looking out a window, enjoying casual chat, feeling for Adele? Where has that tight-lipped, fidgety woman gone? Her splintered heart has been smoothed.

It occurs to me that this is some sort of rite of passage. I text my friend Caro, 'In Relationship Challenge #52: buying clothes together.'

Laden with ribbon-handled shopping bags we catch the bus back to my flat, struck dumb by shopping torpor, heading for Relationship Challenge #53.

I elbow the door open and step in Harry's shit. Also, look, there is a tear in the sofa, ragged little teeth marks around its edges. Shreds of deep burnt orange dangle from Harry's unrepentant mouth.

Is there any easy, undetectable way to dispose of Harry? He has crossed an indisputable line now.

I'm trapped, not wanting to move my shoe and make another blob of shit. Samuel, stuck in the doorway, unable to see my dilemma, pushes me forward a little. My foot slides on the boards, I lose balance and fall. Even as I fall, I wonder whether Samuel will go to his dog, or to me.

He drops his bags and picks me up, holds me tight and croons 'You're ok. You're ok' then releases one hand to stroke my head. I lean into him and close my eyes. I hear Harry's nails tap tap over, and a wet little tongue licks my hand.

To my mind, that's Relationship Challenges #53-110 hurdled in one.

About the author

Kathy Prokhovnik writes fiction (long form, short stories, microfiction) and nonfiction. She is currently finalising her second novel and preparing a podcast series about Sydney. She blogs at kathyprokhovnik.com

Author's insights

'This story is based on true events, just not in that order or with those connections. Firstly, I was in the men's section of David Jones in the early stages of a new relationship (with 'Samuel'), and I texted a friend, as documented. Adele was singing, slightly distorted. Secondly, I had minded a friend's dog who would shit on the floor in revenge for being left behind. These images were in my mind, along with the astonishment, confusion, delight of managing a new relationship two years after the death of my husband. So, basically, a mashup.'

Ed's comments

This author has mastered the art of 'showing, not telling.' Rather than relying on description and exposition, Kathy brings her characters and their desires to life by manifesting them in the real world. For example, the 'Relationship Challenges' (which reveal so much about character) are not presented merely as a thought in the protagonist's head, but as a text message sent to a friend.

Each detail – the dog, the shopping trip, the song that is playing in the background – is selected with intention and purpose and woven together in a way that develops both character and plot, whilst keeping the story dynamic and grounded in the present. We learn all we need to know about Samuel from the way he describes himself, and how he treats his dog. Even something as mundane as a sofa becomes the keystone of the story: at first an act of rebellion, then a romantic venue, and finally a catalyst for jealousy and reconciliation.

Amanda's comments

This story offers us another great example of how writing and plot can work together to deliver a compelling piece of flash fiction.

In my view, this particular story's strength lies in the careful selection of small details, such as the distorted Adele music, and the burnt orange sofa.

Although this piece went with the more direct approach to the 'crossing the line' and 'rite' prompts, it nevertheless delivered a strong hook, an impactful and engaging plot, and a very satisfying conclusion. It was a delight to read.

UNTITLED #2

Greg Schmidt

Amanda sat anxiously on the toilet surveying the cubicle walls. A large piece of graffiti, jaggedly scratched in the back of the door stared down at her, demanding to be read.

> PERFORM THE RITE
> DROP YE BREEKS
> AND TAKE A SHITE

Charming, she thought. She tore a square of toilet paper from the roll and folded it idly in her hands as she attended to her business.

Not one to venture into public toilets, particularly for the longer form of the task, Amanda was keen to be away from this place. She preferred the sanctity of her own facilities.

Her friends teased her when she spoke of her reluctance to use public toilets.

'The world won't turn to shit,' they mocked. 'What's the worst that could happen?'

Exposure to the bountiful bacteria-rich surfaces for starters, primarily the ungodly one upon which she now perched.

Today though, the need outweighed all else so here she sat, atop a stinking shopping mall public toilet, urging herself to finish quickly.

When the transaction was complete, she stood, pulled up her breeks – to use the local parlance – and flushed.

The pipes clanked and churned loudly. Above, the fluorescent lights faintly flickered.

Amanda opened the cubicle door ready to wash her hands and wash this experience from her mind, only to be greeted by a man leaning against the sink. If his appearance in the ladies' toilets wasn't shocking enough, he was dressed in a kilt, luxuriant in red and green tartan.

'Did ye perform the rite, lassie?' he said fervently in a thick Scottish accent.

'What?' stammered Amanda, keeping her distance. 'Who are you? This is the ladies' room.'

'This place be cursed, should the rite be complete.'

'Rite? What are you talking about? Get out of here or I'll call security.'

Amanda moved towards the door, but the man quickly blocked her way. The words of her friends echoed in her mind. Frontrunner now for the worst thing that could happen in a public toilet was being assaulted by some Scottish weirdo.

'Look mister,' she said, finding venom in her voice, 'I don't know who you think you—'

'Jus' answer me lass' he said, ignoring her. 'Did yer skin touch that unholy seal and did ye leave something behind?'

'I beg your pardon!'

'Did ye put yer bum on that seat and...' he said, motioning towards the cubicle.

'Well, yes, that's generally how these things work,' she said absentmindedly, shocked at being asked such a question.

'But it's no business of yours,' she continued, regathering her composure.

'Ah lass,' he said forlornly. 'In completing the rite ye broke the seal and crossed a line betwixt worlds.'

'What!' scoffed Amanda.

'The world ye ken is gone.'

'Right,' she said, having had enough of this. 'Quite the pleasure listening to your ramblings, now out of my way.'

'Ye dinnae wanna go oot there, lass.'

Amanda pushed past the man, purposefully striding through the door, back out into the mall. The scene before her so overwhelmed her senses that it took a moment to register.

Every surface, every object within sight, was smeared in a sludgy, brown, moist muck. The floor, like a syrupy bog, sucked at her feet and she sank as she tried to steady her balance. Above hung dark slimy stalactites from which dripped small brown blobs, landing on the floor with squelchy splashes.

A putrid smell penetrated her nose, invading her insides, as she breathed in.

'It's all…' gasped Amanda, struggling to find words, to find air.

'Aye lass,' said the man emerging behind her, ''tis all shite.'

About the author

Greg Schmidt is an aspiring writer from Western Sydney. His short stories have featured in the 2024 *Westwords Living Stories Prize* and the *Lane Cove Literary Awards 2023*, but he is most proud of the praise for a little story about poo.

Author's insights

'I don't know from what recesses of my mind this ludicrous story sprang, but I do know what inspired me to not give up on it. *Not Quite Write* had a podcast with tips on how to win the competition, and one piece of advice was something like "If you want to write a ridiculous and disgusting story, then you've come to the right place". When I was worried this story was becoming too silly for a competition, I remembered that, and just ran with it.'

Ed's comments

Comedy can be risky, because you're never sure if your personal tastes will translate to a wider audience. But this one is hilarious!

I loved the author's dedication to the sheer absurdity of the premise. The idea of a public toilet that is inhabited by a supernatural Scotsman certainly cannot be accused of being cliché. And the final, memorable line really sticks the landing.

Amanda's comments

This story delivered both shits AND giggles. I'm not exaggerating when I say that laughing at this story caused me physical pain!

When I first read the story, I wasn't sure if Greg intentionally set out to name his character after me (with my surname featured prominently too), but it certainly helped me to connect to the story, and no doubt made it all the funnier.

Comedy is bloody hard to do well, particularly in a competition against more 'elegant' pieces, but this author did it *very* well.

2023 LONGLIST

The following list represents the remaining longlisted entries, in no particular order:

- PITCH (IMP)ERFECT by John Ho
- SHARE THE LOVE by Tash Bonynge
- THE ICON by Matthew Malcolm
- PEOPLE RAIN AND STREET JAZZ by Glenn Holmes
- FAREWELL TO THEE, PRECIOUS BALLS by Galen Gower
- MINNIE, THE EXTREMELY STRONG RUNNER by Kay Rae Chomic
- HOW TO ESTABLISH CORDIAL RELATIONS WITH YOUR CEPHALOPOD NEIGHBOUR by Mairead Robinson
- BABYSITTING FOR YOUR OLDER SISTER RIGHT AFTER YOUR BOYFRIEND BREAKS UP WITH YOU by Sheila M.
- FAST TIMES IN FAST CARS by Deanna Duxbury

- THE STRATHKELLAR LIGHTS by Susan Mclaughlin
- LONGING FOR HOME by Jo Skinner
- CAKE DUDE… by Liv Hibbitt
- PUNK ROCK MIRAGE by Punk Rock Nanny
- REST by Tatum
- WILD HUNT HOMECOMING by E. M. Nikolaev
- JUST DESSERTS by Chris Cottom
- SATURDAY UMBRELLA by George Mackenzie
- PURSUED, TRIVIALLY by Ruth Lord
- BRITENEE'S BAD DAY by Greg Eccleston
- UNFORTUNATELY, FORTUNATELY by Sally Simon
- TRAIN STATION by Miah Sandvik
- A DANDELION PUFF by Sara Chansarkar
- DOUG VS THE IMMORTAL SNAIL by Freya King
- THE WAY OF DINOSAURS by Em Allen
- SLOWLY by Iris Joo
- ALWAYS, OFTEN, SOMETIMES, RARELY, NEVER by Olive Alvis
- HAT FACTORY BLUES by Dominic Kenny
- A PARTICULAR AFTERNOON by R. C. Barajas
- HANGMAN by Edgar Lavoie
- THE CODA by Elizabeth Schild
- GUESS WHO? by Lisa Harper Campbell
- STRIKE ACTION by Michael Burrows
- SOUTHERN BAPTISM by Kathryn Healy
- WHAT FRANNY DID by Isabelle Berns
- LOVE IS BLIND by Christy Roth

- WOMAN, NON-ENGLISH SPEAKING BACKGROUND by Iris Joo
- SENSORY by Drew Reynolds
- LET'S SING GHAZALS AT NIGHT by Abhishek Sengupta
- THEY SAID THAT WE by Shuen Chan
- FIFTY FIFTY by Frances Greenleaf
- LIMERENCE by JM Hooijer
- PARADISE LOST by Jayne Rice
- WINNING SCIENTIFICALLY by Pam Makin
- WORTH THE SOUL by Kjanela Fawcett
- UNDER THE HAMMER by Bob Topping
- TRICKSTER by Taylor O'Connell
- TRAFFICKING WISH-CRAFT by M. Lea Gray
- THE PRIVILEGE by Chandler Ahart
- THE ROBOT by Emma Harrowing
- FRED AND I by Alex Frank
- SHALLOW BREATHING by Christina Wilson
- THE LAST BITE by Gabi Taylor
- PERFECTLY. WELL, ADEQUATELY. by Terence Gallagher
- BEER INN by Annie Louisa

JANUARY 2024

Overview

The January 2024 *Not Quite Write Prize for Flash Fiction* challenged writers to create an original piece of fiction of no more than 500 words, which:

included the word **PUNCH**.

included the action **'spilling something'**.

broke the writing rule **'avoid clichés'**.

The competition drew **257** entries from authors in **23** countries around the world. That's **125,778** words for our judges, Ed and Amanda, to read. That's about the same number of words as a **Jane Austen novel**.

Please enjoy the following top six stories from this round of the competition...

IT NEVER RAINS BUT IT POURS

Athena Law

Moist. Just wanted to get that one out of the way, but I know you've probably curled your lip and flared your nostrils after reading it. Me, I love the word and the feeling, the very idea of it, but what I love most is rain. Heavy, pounding, relentless rain.

Here in the humid tropics, amongst the palm trees, the rain spills from the skies for weeks. I don't let it dampen my spirits, quite the opposite – I rejoice – it doesn't take long before everything is moist. Ceilings, walls, clothes, skin. The tourists battle against the wet, but I don't need to anymore. I shower in my clothes then lie on the bed under my ceiling fan, relishing the whap-whap-whap of the blades sluicing through heavy air.

I'm the person who stands too close behind you in the supermarket queue. Nobody notices the short lady in the straw hat and red sunglasses, just a harmless local. But whenever I spot a bare, tanned back in the middle of summer I sidle near enough to touch it.

Sometimes I think my heart bangs so loud in my chest that you'll hear it. My palms are damp with need, fingers itching to draw a trail through the fine drops of sweat beading across the oily slick of your shoulder blade.

And you? You can be anybody, I'm not fussy.

Where else can I find you? It goes without saying it must be somewhere private, just for us. The idea arrives with blinding simplicity, and I prepare with care.

I relish the overnight wait, deep in the rainforest, car windows open. I hear the final flurries of birds settling in before the nocturnal creatures come out to play. All around, the lush drip-drip-drip of wetness sliding off vines and leaves, down to the pungent forest floor.

It's early when I hear you coming. I slide from the car, peeling my thighs from the sweaty seat, and step onto the track. What do you see emerging from the trees, in the pale dawn light? Only a short lady in a straw hat, harmless. But it's what I see that makes my heart thud, and my palms damp. There's two of you.

We're told to look after tourists, that they're the lifeblood of our isolated town. Am I not simply upholding my civic duty to warn backpackers of the predatory crocodile which took a fisherman at this very spot yesterday? Am I not caring enough to ferry you back to the safety of my own home?

I pour you both glasses of sweet iced tea, for the shock. The old ceiling fan punches through the humidity, causing darling goosebumps across your golden, youthful skin. It's a mere moment before you slump in your chairs, staring at me in mute bewilderment.

'Cat got your tongues?' I ask caringly, as I drag you into your new bedroom.

And now, we're all going to live happily ever after.

About the author

Athena Law's natural habitat is her cosy study, where she can be found at midnight bashing away at her beleaguered keyboard. She's currently obsessed with collecting excellent pencils, adores a good comma splice sentence, and G&Ts are her kryptonite.

Author's insights

'When you live in Queensland you know there's going to be hot wet summers and not in a good way. Occasionally it rains for weeks and during one such deluge I was driving between work appointments with frizzy hair and soggy shoes and felt decidedly moist. I hate that word, who doesn't? It occurred to me I could start a story with the M word, but the story would take an unexpected turn where we'd meet someone who relishes in it. So two lines on my notes app taken on that day sparked into life once I received the *Not Quite Write* prompts!'

Ed's comments

Our winning entry is positively dripping with tension. The moisture is palpable, seeping from every pore, crack and crevice. It feels as though slimy, sweaty fingers are drawing the reader towards the story's chilling climax: a twisted take on a classic fairy-tale ending (and a gratifying use of the anti-prompt).

Beware the short lady in the straw hat!

Amanda's comments

This story displayed originality of concept, and an incredibly strong sense of character which had me hooked from the very first word.

What I found most satisfying was how it ramped up, using evocative snapshots to enhance that sense of disquiet such as, 'I shower in my clothes then lie on the bed under my ceiling fan,' and 'whenever I spot a bare, tanned back in the middle of summer I sidle near enough to touch it,' and 'darling goosebumps across your golden, youthful skin.' It's an excellent example of Poe's *Single Effect Theory*, in which every part of the story – including that first word – is being used to evoke a single, unified emotion in the reader.

The word and action prompts are seamlessly woven into the prose, and the anti-prompt is evidenced in the title forming the inspiration for the entire narrative.

This story is anything but cliché.

BLESS THIS MESS

Chad Frame

Dawn breaks like a dropped jar of marmalade
over night's black marble counter. And yet—
it really happened. I'm standing here, half-

lit in the kitchen, half-asleep, dumbstruck
by strewn, sticky shards of everything
that once made sense. Then I remember why

it no longer does. You've been gone three years,
and every morning in the small space
between night and day, sleep and wakefulness,

fragile glass jar and unyielding surface,
I almost forget. **Ignorance is Bliss**,
the cliché printed on the stretched canvas

once hung in the hall with all your garish
mass-market home store decor. All gone, now.
Sometimes I forget. But I remember

how we met—the personal you posted,
Looking for someone to swap secrets with,
two strangers in a padded booth sharing

greasy spoon breakfast and the absolute
worst thing we'd ever done. It was easy
to confide in someone who didn't know

anyone I knew, whose lips were studded
with toast crumbs glued on by smeared marmalade.
I told you about the time I ignored

a stray dog whining for food, its old eyes
rheumy as fogged headlights, how the next day
I drove by its crushed body in the road,

those same eyes still open. You wiped your mouth
with a cheap napkin, looked me in the eyes,
and told me you'd hit something with your car

one night when you'd glanced away from the road
to check your phone. We asked for the check, left,
decided your apartment was closer,

and an hour later, we took turns on top
of one another while an **I'd Rather
Be Knitting** throw pillow watched from the chair

in the corner. 'Would you really?' I asked
in the afterglow, nodding to the throw.
'Do you want the truth?' you smirked, lying there

curled in the circle of my arms. 'Always,'

I murmured, kissing the top of your head.
But this morning, I'm alone with my mess

of a life, what once was a half-full jar
now a crushed wreck on the floor and counter,
streaks and gobs of orange everywhere.

By habit, I reach for the **Bless This Mess**
tea towel tucked through the door of the stove,
but it's gone. You're gone. I have a secret

I haven't told—I knew you'd be driving
when I texted **I love you**, knew you might
not resist looking and answering back.

You punched the brakes too late. They'd wheeled you off
by the time I arrived. There was still glass
everywhere. There was blood, sticky-sweet

as streaks of jam. **Everything happens
for a reason**, yes, I know. A woman
appears behind me with paper towels.

'My husband says if he catches you here
one more time he'll call the cops.' Finger held
to my lips, I open the sliding door,

quiet as a roadside body, slip out
the way I came into secretless dawn,
and leave the house I lost when I lost you.

About the author

Chad Frame is a poet who uses fiction to sneakily write poetry and poetry to sneakily tell stories. He's the author of three books and published in a bunch of places including the actual Moon. Yes, really.

Chad's work features twice in this anthology. You can find his other contribution at page 105.

Author's insights

'Bless This Mess is a narrative poem in the style I've become known for — decasyllabic tercets. As a poet, it was the easiest and most familiar way for me to write, so that came naturally. I started with the line about dawn breaking like a dropped jar of marmalade because the image had been stuck in my head, and the prompt of "spilling something" got me going. The reason I chose the form in the first place was in response to a few statements by the *Not Quite Write* judges mentioning being biased against poetry, and that while it wasn't forbidden as an entry, a poem submitted to the contest would have almost no chance winning. Well, challenge accepted.'

Ed's comments

We are as surprised as you are to see a poem take the number two spot! Well done, Chad, for challenging and obliterating our preconceptions.

I love how effortlessly the narrative twists its serpentine course through past and present, infused with unnerving little details and half-cloaked motifs which hint at a deeper meaning.

We are not permitted everything we desire to know about this relationship, but shouldn't a good poem evoke more than it explains?

Amanda's comments

Once again, poetry has woven its way into my heart... and into second place!

Now, I'm no poet, so 'decasyllabic tercets' are foreign territory to me, but this story reads equally well (if not better) as prose. It sings with vivid details that paint a picture of an entire relationship in fewer than 500 words – no mean feat!

The use of cliché in the form of home décor was an original and fitting take on the anti-prompt, and the specific choice of cliché phrases adds a layer of meaning just under the surface.

If I had to critique anything, I would have liked to better understand the protagonist's motivation for causing their loved one's death. However, this perceived weakness is offset by a satisfying circularity to the story, with each thread weaving its way through to find its place in the resolution.

AS FAR AS THE EYE CAN SEE

Tess Allen

Five seconds. Maybe 10. That was all it took. I'd closed my eyes. After another sleep disturbed night. When I'd looked up, she was gone.

Now, my throat tightens as if compressed by invisible hands. Sand flies as I leap from my towel. Blue sky has been replaced by grey. White-tipped waves crash as my eyes dart down the shoreline. To my left there's the lighthouse, to my right it's just beach as far as the eye can see. The few other families dotted along the sand seem unmoved by, or unaware of, my panic. Kids with sand-covered legs donning wide-brimmed hats play.

I race to a family nearby. 'My daughter! I can't find her. Have you seen her?' I shriek.

The woman stands. Behind dark sunglasses her expression is a mix of confusion and concern. 'No, sorry. What's she wearing?'

What was she wearing? Her favourite rainbow bathers? Her flamingo hat? My thoughts, like a maelstrom, swirl. I shake my head, lost for words.

Instead, I sprint to the water's edge. 'Lucy!! Lucy, where are you?'

I try to swallow, mouth parched. 'Lucy!' I croak. Feeling a warm hand on my bare shoulder, I turn to see the woman beside me.

'What's she wearing? How old is she?' she asks.

I close my eyes and exhale, pushing the words out. 'A flamingo hat. Blue bathers,' I say. 'She's only four!' Hot tears spill down my cheeks.

'I'll get help.' she says rushing back to her kids. The youngest wraps chubby arms around her mother's legs.

I double over holding my stomach as if I've been punched. This can't be happening. I look back towards our towels. Laid out side by side. Lucy's sand toys beside them. A pink shovel protruding from the yellow bucket.

I rack my brain, recalling the morning. We'd walked from our beach house. Along the row of peppermint trees, their bare, brown trunks lining the path, then past the ice-cream kiosk. Flipflops flicking sand as Lucy ran, giggling, along the track bucket in hand. There was no breeze then. The ocean flat, an inviting aquamarine.

Seagulls squawk bringing me back to the present. I stare at the lighthouse. A beacon. With its red and white stripes, Lucy had said it looked like a candy cane. Standing, I run. My forearms tingle as the sun beats down. Piles of seaweed line the beach, matted brown tangles rotting. I run until my lungs force me to stop. Chest heaving, I pause.

'Candice!' I turn to see my husband, Paul, rushing towards me.

'You found her?', I ask. When he reaches me, he won't meet my eyes. Silent as he pulls me into his arms. I push back. 'Where is she?'

'Honey, let's get you home.' Fingernails dig in as he grasps my shoulders, guiding me up the path. Past the ice-cream kiosk, along the row of peppermint trees, brown trunks lined with posters. I see the photograph. Read the words.

Missing.

Reward offered.

Lucy Morgan Age 4.

About the author

Tess Allen is a creative writer who resides in Boorloo/Perth. When she's not working, or juggling family commitments, she can be found percolating a story or scene over a cup of coffee. She is currently working on her first long-form project: a domestic suspense story set in London.

Author's insights

'I was on holiday in Albany, a town on the south coast of WA at the time of the January *Not Quite Write Prize*. I started a few other stories, but nothing was feeling right. A morning run along the shell-covered white sandy beaches where the chilly, blue waters of the Southern Ocean lap on the shore, I realised I had a perfect story setting. I often get inspiration from my stories by thinking of 'What if...' – a worst nightmare for any parent is losing their child but there have been countless stories written about that and I love to write stories with a twist. The "avoid clichés" anti-prompt gave me just what I needed to formulate my story's twist.'

Ed's comments

The narrator's abrupt sentences emphasise the urgency and desperation of this highly fraught scenario. The feeling of rising panic is contagious, while the narrative eye twitches from detail to fleeting detail before finally settling on one that throws the entire story into a new light.

Tess has written a highly memorable story, and one that packs an emotional 'punch'.

Amanda's comments

What stood out to me about this story was its emotional pull. From the first read and with each re-read, I am gripped by this mother's distress over the loss of her child. A trail of breadcrumbs leads us to the final twist, evoking that satisfying 'aha' moment when the truth is finally revealed.

The author draws the reader into the scene with vivid details, such as, 'The youngest wraps chubby arms around her mother's legs,' and 'With its red and white stripes, Lucy had said it looked like a candy cane.'

As far as the prompts are concerned, this story shows how keeping it simple can sometimes be the best solution.

A FUNNY STORY

Dean Koorey

Line dancing night at the Laughing Fox and all the usual lines were in attendance.

Jaw, Plunging Neck and Visible Panty were busy taking selfies at the bar as Receding Hair looked on forlornly. In a corner booth, Land and On were having their usual high pitched screaming match, while Bathroom banged on the door for Coke to come out. A typical evening.

At table four, Pickup returned to his friends, trio of drinks in hand. 'No luck with "Jamaican me crazy,"' he reported above the country music.

'There must be an easier way,' pondered Stream, taking two of the glasses, and handing one to Punch.

'Anyone know any good jokes?' Punch asked.

The other two groaned.

'We're not setting you up anymore!' barked Pickup, spilling some of his drink. 'You always ruin them! Remember Rabbi?... Kiwi?... Knock Knock?'

'Hey, she was a stalker! Kept turning up at my door.'

'Okay, maybe not her. But what about that cute Irish joke?'

'Look, we just weren't compatible. Although her Dad liked me...'

'Of course he liked you, he's a Dad Joke and you're a lame punchline!'

Punch flinched. 'I'm just old-fashioned. Besides, what's wrong with, 'Why the long face?''

Pickup and Stream exchanged glances just as Tag appeared, all sweat and smiles, boot scooting off the dance floor.

'I'm lovin' it!' she announced, flopping into a chair. 'Got milk?'

Plot also emerged from the throng.

'Is this night going anywhere or what?' she asked the folk of table four.

They shrugged.

'Ugh, okay I'm going to hang out with Clothes and Pipe – he always has plans. Picket's already waiting out front. Who's in?'

Pickup and Stream literally jumped at the chance, waving their goodbyes.

'You sure you don't wanna go with them?' Punch asked his friend.

'Think different,' Tag replied, and they sipped in Shania-Twain-tinged silence.

A blonde appeared collecting empties, tray in hand.

'Why the long face?' Punch offered.

'I'm not that kind of joke!' she scowled and marched off.

Punch sighed. 'Maybe I do need to change my ways...'

'Eat fresh?'

'Yeah Tag, maybe. I always thought I'd find the right Joke, we'd have a few laughs, nothing serious...'

'Because you're worth it.' Tag nodded sagely.

And that's when Punch saw her.

Across the crowded dance floor.

Swaying to the music near the door.

All jokes aside, could this be the one?

'Holy shit,' Punch ventriloquised. 'I think I have to go...'

'Just do it!' Tag squealed.

He leapt up, just as the line dancers moved in right-angled unison – creating an instant wall of denim and tassels. Trapped, Punch lost sight of her.

'Go around, honey!' called Bee from the line.

But by the time he reached the door, she was gone.

Punch scanned the bar. Nothing.

Outside, Punch stared out at the dark street, defeated, to a muffled twangy soundtrack.

It began to rain.

Perfect.

A boot scraped against the pavement behind him.

He turned.

She smiled. Then she spoke.

'A horse walks into a bar...'

About the author

Dean is a New Zealand-born, Australian-based, starry-eyed freelance copywriter who loves short stories so much that he co-created Furious Fiction in 2018 – probably inspiring *Not Quite Write* in the process. He has three freshly matured children and when not writing anthology-worthy pieces, you'll find him solving cryptic crosswords in his favourite café. Find out more at deankoorey.com.

Dean's work features twice in this anthology. You can find his other contribution at page 153.

Author's insights

'This was my first ever *Not Quite Write* piece and used the "punch" prompt to tell a cliché meet-cute with a difference! I initially had fun coming up with "line" gags, but the challenge was injecting a story with heart into what would otherwise have just been a surreal conveyor belt of (literal) one-liners. I was proud of how it all came out and clearly it should have won – who are these judges anyway?'

Ed's comments

This is a superbly executed concept, brimming with clever wordplay, which continues to reveal additional layers upon repeated reading.

Despite the entire cast being comprised of a collection of anthropomorphised, abstract concepts, Dean manages not only to imbue each with a distinct (and appropriate) personality, but also delivers a satisfying plot, complete with happy ending.

Amanda's comments

What can I say? I love a pun! This story had me laughing out loud from the first read, and still gets me every time.

What this story does better than some other comedies, is find a way to go beyond the surface level humour to tell a human story too. In this case, we have a romance, with a protagonist we can't help but feel for, so we can only cheer when he finally gets his girl (joke?) in the end!

THE WAY OF THE BINS

Bob Topping

It was my dull idea to clobber and bag the feral cat, and the odour is foul. My wife tells me to go. Not our wheelie bin, she says, or the neighbour's, so by default it's the beach.

The wobbly bag smacks my thigh as I fast-paced down Coleman's Lane, along its dark and lonely length. Twelve steps, and I'm past the last house to reach the first set of bins. Clustered in pairs, their prominent red lids nestle under a pole offering lemony light. They're clamped to deter the likes of me but I sausage-shape the bag and squeeze it through the circular cutout on the lid. It slides like jelly and the smell lingers as I retreat a step or two into a fearful stillness, like the watching shadows are all alone and trapped in sleep.

I didn't notice the old man by the other set of bins. A shabby figure, scarcely distinct, shaking scrappy shopping bags where the walkways seem to disappear. My wife says he haunts the parks, hovering over the bins in the afternoons when she's jogging the beach path with the girls, his grey hair all but hidden under a shapeless hat. He's half-human, she says, and there's lice by the funny manner he scratches his scalp as they pass.

'They say he whistles at the birds and barks at the dogs. Don't stare or he'll hiss. His sore eyes suck you in I've been told. We give him a wide berth.' Her shoulders shivered as she spoke.

He hasn't heard my approach, or if he had, there's no sudden twist or turn or drop of his soiled bags. He is leaning over a bin, awkwardly, one scrawny arm punching like a piston through the hole in the lid. Probably, I shouldn't look but he is a good distance away and I slink back behind my bins. Something is there, spilling from his bin, and the something I see is raw skin and torn, a feathered frame. The shape loosens and flaps and struggles in his clenched hand. It stretches a wing, and he releases a leg. There is a burst of words, a garble I don't recognise.

The bird looks like ruffled roadkill, a magpie. It opens its beak wide and preens. The old man rubs his hand along the bird's back and jerks its timid head from side to side in motion to his own, and he grunts, and it tweets.

And then the bird is gone, and I feel afraid if I move, he'll turn and come by me, but he clasps a grubby bag and tilts his head in my direction and fingers the air. Beach walkers say he stuffs the bags with feathers of dead gulls, sucks their bones and disappears in the sea mists before morning light.

I watch the old man start up the walkway, head down and shaking like he was crying, and wonder how could they all be so sure?

About the author

Bob Topping is a retired teacher who lives in rural south-eastern Queensland. He enjoys his AFL and gardening and writes short stories drawn from characters encountered across this wide and diverse country.

Author's insights

'There is a pathway near Bulli Beach between two scenic headlands frequented by walkers, joggers and bike-riders, and a scrawny, bare-footed, grey-whiskered man who is often spied scavenging among the rubbish bins. He avoids conversation and eyes of others, and vice versa, like a living cliché of repulsion. This made a way into a short story on how we may relate to others and how wrong we can be.'

Note: This story was resubmitted with edits for this anthology.

Ed's comments

An unsettling mix of the familiar and the creepy, this story achieves its nightmarish quality by casting a shadow over the line between the real and imagined.

It elevates each mildly grotesque detail. Feathers. Teeth. Things that squish and squawk and ooze.

This story left me with an overwhelming desire to wash my hands.

Amanda's comments

It's so rewarding to see stories in which the author clearly took inspiration from one or more of the prompts to create something unique. In this case, we start with our cliché of 'letting the cat out of the bag,' and things quickly get weird.

What I loved most about this piece was how it grabbed my attention and pulled me deep into the scene. There's something so frighteningly relatable about this character trying to destroy the evidence of his worst behaviour. I couldn't look away.

What I felt this story perhaps lacked was a plot in which the beginning, middle and end weave together into a cohesive whole. Nevertheless, it's a lesson in how evocative and original details can lift a story out of the pack.

THE EARLY BIRD CATCHES THE WORM

Anne Wilkins

Nana collects sayings. She's got one for every kinda situation. This morning, she's trying to wake Daisy and I, and she's at the end of our bed, pullin' our covers off, telling us the early bird catches the worm. Daisy and I just want to sleep, and we don't want to catch worms, but there's no stopping Nana.

'C'mon. Get a move on, sleepyheads.'

We tumble out of bed to the bathroom, while Nana makes our bed. She doesn't stop talking, even though Daisy and I have stopped listening. Mama used to say that Nana could talk the hind legs off a donkey when she got goin', and she's definitely goin' this morning.

Nana's got lots of nice things in her bathroom. Trinkets, she calls them. There's a little white clamshell that holds soap, a coloured fish, and fluffy towels. The soap smells like you can eat it. Daisy picks it up, but it's stuck to the clamshell and the next thing you know, the clamshell falls to the floor and breaks into two halves. Daisy bursts into tears, and Nana comes in, all in a flutter.

'Let's see. What's the problem, sweetheart?' She picks up the broken clamshell. 'Why, this old thing? I'd been meaning to replace that. In fact, you've done me a favour, Daisy.'

Nana wipes Daisy's tears and gives her a hug. I'm sorta feeling left out, just standing there, watching their two halves hugging, like a mend. I'm almost wishing it had been me that had broken something when Nana sees my face.

'Oh, come on in, pet.' She pulls me into her arms for one of her great bear hugs. And I get to crying too. Not about the clamshell, but about the other broken things.

After breakfast, Daisy and I ask about the worms we're meant to be catching. Nana laughs and tells us it's a saying, but that we can help in the garden. Nana's garden is just like her bathroom. All fancy. She's even got a butterfly shed where she takes all the caterpillars and gives them a good, safe home till they're hatched from their cocoons and can fly away. Nana's good at looking after things, keeping them safe.

Mama comes back from the hospital early the next morning. Her right eye is all black and blue from the punch that slipped from Daddy.

Mama spills out her tears and Nana's doling out one of her bear hugs.

'Keep them safe, just a bit longer,' Mama whispers. 'Till I get things sorted.'

'It'll be all right, dove,' says Nana. 'Tomorrow's a new day.'

After Mama's gone, Daisy and I curl up like caterpillars on Nana's couch, not ready to fly. Nana tells us a whole can of worms has been opened up, and that the worm has turned. Daisy and I don't know what any of that means, but I heard Nana call Mama a dove before, and I'm hoping the early bird is finally going to catch that worm.

About the author

Anne Wilkins is a sleep-deprived primary school teacher in New Zealand, who writes in her spare time (which she has very little of). Her love of writing is fuelled by copious amounts of coffee, reading and hope. For more information visit www.annewilkinsauthor.com or follow her on facebook.com/annewilkinsauthor

Author's insights

'The Nana in this story has elements of my own Mum who sadly passed away in 2024. Some of the phrases, the trinkets in the bathroom, and the Nana not wanting the children to worry about the broken clamshell are all my Mum. The caterpillars are me, something we've raised. And the domestic violence is something I saw a lot of when I was a family lawyer and the terrible effects it had on families.

'Some of the sayings are so old fashioned and are hard for children to understand these days, and I wanted to explore that. I decided to tie it all together with a cliché, and the best one was: "The early bird catches the worm."'

Ed's comments

Anne has whisked up the anti-prompt and baked it right into the core of her story, like one of Nana's homemade pies.

The recurring clichés and references to doves, caterpillars and broken things take on a metaphorical significance, adding depth and resonance to the child narrator's story – a story that she, thanks to Nana, is fortunately still too innocent to understand.

Amanda's comments

It's the voice that makes this story special. It's the kind of story you can 'hear' as you read it, with dialogue that feels authentic and, ironically, not so cliché when viewed from the perspective of a child.

This story was one in which a straightforward approach to the anti-prompt worked well. We see the cliché phrases being attributed to Nana, and worms and caterpillars featuring throughout to tie the narrative together.

JANUARY 2024 LONGLIST

The following list represents the remaining longlisted entries, in no particular order:

- **WILDCARD WINNER** – STICK IT TO THE MAN by Carla Connolly
- **WILDCARD WINNER** – REBEL REBEL by Ella Micallef
- WORDS LEFT UNSAID by Liv Hibbitt
- ALL IN A DAY'S WORK by Katelyn Phillips
- ANNABELLE IRVING by Lara Cain Gray
- TGIF by Courtney Brown
- THE FLOWER DUET by Fleassy Malay
- TO THE ENDS OF THE WORLD by Anna Hughes
- A BONE OF CONTENTION by Sandra Thom-Jones
- A HAUNTING by Clio Davidson-Lynch
- SENSELESS TRAGEDY by Rachael Crane
- IT GOES WITHOUT SAYING by Madeline Howard
- THE ATTRACTION by Philippa Freegard
- A LOVE AT FIRST SIGHT by Jaden Christopher
- OLD POISONS by Franky Seymour

- PARADISE by Ajay Sabhaney
- MEMORY LANE by Shannon Mackie
- ASHES TO ASHES, DUST TO DUST by Marissa Hanley
- SPHERICAL REFRACTION by Jacqueline Koshorst
- THE WEATHER IN ERIE, PENNSYLVANIA by Mathew Peters
- EXPOSURE by Anneloes Barth
- EVERYTHING IN AUSTRALIA IS TRYING TO KILL YOU by Timothy Hayes
- THE CIRCLE OF LIFE by The Wayward Scribe
- THE HARICOT CALICO, OR CAT GOT YOUR TONGUE by Sam James
- FLOAT LIKE A BUTTERFLY by Katie Challis
- A BUN IN THE OVEN by Zelda C. Thorne
- MAGIC by Melissa Stigall
- TETHERED by Kat Habermann
- WHISPERS by Trey Dowell
- FIVE DAYS LATE IS BETTER THAN FOREVER by Sarah Hurd
- LIKE A MOTH TO A FLAME by Camsyn Clair
- TWO BUCKETS AND A ROPE by Thom Brodkin
- FUNERAL RITES by Patrick Moon
- SALT OF THE EARTH by Karen Mitani

Note: Since 2024, each judge has awarded a wildcard prize to an entry which did not make the shortlist but which we otherwise felt deserved recognition.

APRIL 2024

Overview

The April 2024 *Not Quite Write Prize for Flash Fiction* challenged writers to create an original piece of fiction of no more than 500 words, which:

included the word **DATE**.

included the action **'picking a winner'**.

broke the writing rule **'always use said'**.

The competition drew **212 entries** from authors in **20 countries** around the world. That's **100,497** words for our judges, Ed and Amanda, to read. That's about the same number of words as *To Kill a Mockingbird* by **Harper Lee**.

Please enjoy the following top six stories from this round of the competition...

UNSAY ANYTHING

Chad Frame

'Maybe I will,' I unsaid, and felt my hand again on your cheek, smoothing the red welt I'd just left. My arm pulled back.

'So why don't you take it all back, then?' you unsaid.

'I wish I'd never chosen you,' I unsaid, and backed away from you into the doorway, tears snaking back up my face to vanish into the corners of my eyes.

'You swore for better or worse,' you unsaid, and the picture frame lifted off the bedroom floor and back into your hand, the fractal glass shards fitting back into place like a seamless puzzle.

In the frame, behind the glass, we were embracing. Young, newlywed, naïve. Your face, unshadowed by stubble, undaunted by drink. My eyes, uncircled by darkness.

'We never fucking were,' I unsaid.

'We're not those people anymore,' you unsaid, and set the picture frame down on the bedside table.

'Don't walk away from me when I'm talking to you,' I unsaid. I disappeared from the doorway.

Five years rewound like old film reel.

I unstormed out to my parents' house. You unbecame an alcoholic, your mouth like a Jim Beam factory, filling bottle after bottle with woodcharred bogwater.

I uncaught you. You unfucked your secretary when you thought I was still out at therapy.

You unsaid it was a great idea. I unsaid I was falling apart and needed to talk to a professional.

You unhit the bottle. We unmourned the loss.

I sucked the screams back into my mouth, fell asleep in a pool of clotted blood.

You unwore me down. 'It's a name that works for any gender,' you uninsisted.

You wanted Robin.

We unposted the announcement—caption unwritten, photo untaken. A rattle, a positive test, a tiny pair of shoes, a chalkboard with 'Coming Soon' scrawled in careful cursive. At the corner of each word, the letter tails looped into hearts.

The chalk traced back over the words, unscratched them from the slate. Unetched the hearts. Tabula rasa.

We unmoved into the house. Packed lives back into boxes, loaded them onto the truck, drove them back to our separate apartments where we unSharpied them 'dishes,' 'towels,' 'books.'

We retreated from the altar.

You pulled the ring from my finger. Rose from one knee on a windswept beach.

We vomited dinners back onto plates. Every date unhappened, one by one, undone.

'I choose you,' I untold you, lying in your arms.

I unended things with my college boyfriend.

'I'm sorry,' I untold Adam, tears snaking back up his handsome face to vanish into the corners of his bright eyes. 'I met someone else.'

Adam was the same in both directions. Consistent, loving, stable.

You were unpredictable, exciting, dangerous.

At a party, you unhit on me, dark eyes full of mystery and promise. 'I'm Jake,' you unintroduced yourself, cheeks undimpling as your grin disappeared.

Everything stopped.

Everything moves forward again. 'Fuck off,' I yell over the music when you approach. You don't even get a word out. 'I'm happy with my boyfriend.'

About the author

Chad Frame is a poet who uses fiction to sneakily write poetry and poetry to sneakily tell stories. He's the author of three books and published in a bunch of places including the actual Moon. Yes, really.

Chad's work features twice in this anthology. You can find his other contribution at page 69.

Author's insights

'Unsay Anything was another attempt by me to challenge the editors to consider a nontraditional narrative structure. Here, I was inspired by the anti-prompt of "Just use said" by reasoning that the opposite of "said" isn't some other dialogue tag or even silence -- the opposite of saying something is unsaying it, pulling the words back. While I didn't write a poem like I did with Bless This Mess, this idea of backwards narrative was pulled from a poem of mine, *Nine-Year-Old Suicide in Reverse*, which was first published in *Philadelphia Stories* as a runner-up for the *2019 Sandy Crimmins National Prize for Poetry* and then again as part of my first full length poetry collection, *Little Black Book*. (Fair warning: As sad as you think it is by the title, I promise you it's even sadder when you look up the true story.) 'I was obsessed with the idea of tragedy as this immutable scar on the psyche, but that survivors of traumatic events endlessly replay things in their head, wondering how things could have gone differently, rewinding the sequence of events as if they could be taken back.'

Ed's comments

Our winner has truly embraced the spirit of the anti-prompt with a clever concept that doesn't just tick the boxes.

Every pivotal moment in the implosion of this relationship has been selected for maximum impact, and the arrow drawn from each emotionally-charged exchange back to its causes evokes a feeling of tragic inevitability, like watching a car crash in slow motion.

Amanda's comments

This story burst out of the gate with a bold take on the anti-prompt and did not let up until its breathless conclusion.

While we often advise writers to simplify their writing to create a more satisfying reading experience, this story manages to deliver just the right amount of challenge – offering questions *and* answers to both spark *and* satisfy curiosity.

Domestic violence is a theme we see come up a lot in flash fiction, and this story highlights why. This dramatic slice of life conjures up a whole host of emotions and a chilling insight into lies lived in secret.

It seems Chad is determined to drag us over to the dark side of non-traditional narrative structures and, once again, I am more than happy to be proven wrong!

EVERYONE'S A WINNER

Sam James

I've got bogeys for days. Picking my nose is a bit like hook-a-duck: everyone's a winner.

I really can't stress that enough. I could poke around in there for hours on end and still there would be treasures to find.

My particular penchant used to be to 'go mining' whenever the news was on. You might not remember, but the news used to be so bleak (*The energy crisis continues... Food shortages across the world worsen... There's not enough to go around...*), and I found that picking my nose was a comfort to me.

The women I've dated over the years have found it variously nauseating, repulsive and revolting. The whole gamut of disgust really. But where others saw a gross habit, Lucy saw potential.

'Where does it all come from?' she asked one day. She was pushing the tip of my nose up and staring directly into the depths of my nostrils. 'It's got to come from somewhere. It just doesn't make sense! We should measure it.'

And so, I began to collect the stuff and weigh it. Once, I pulled out more than a kilogram of mucus over the course of a day; there was still more up there when I gave up and went to bed. After that, Lucy's fascination turned to concern, and she took me to see some specialists.

'I'm at a loss to explain your... overabundance,' the ENT doctor admitted, 'but I don't think it's a health risk.'

'I'm similarly stumped,' the biologist added. 'There's simply no anatomical mechanism that could account for that much snot.'

'The laws of thermodynamics suggest this shouldn't be possible. But... I wonder...' wondered the physicist, 'I suppose it might be—we'd have to run some tests.'

So we ran some tests. Endoscopes, MRIs, Geiger counters; there wasn't an instrument available to science that didn't get aimed at my schnoz.

'Do you realise what this means?' Lucy practically bounced when we got the test results back, 'this is going to change the world!' And she was right.

I have a wormhole up my nose.

Why do I have a wormhole up my nose? Where does the other end of the wormhole come out? And why does the other end of the wormhole appear to contain an infinite supply of bogeys? I don't have any of the answers.

But as a result of Lucy's insight, the news is much nicer nowadays. The energy crisis is solved, because we have enough fuel to burn (in the form of dried bogeys). And food shortages are a thing of the past, because we have enough to eat (in the form of 'don't think about it').

For the first time in human history, there's snot enough to go around.

About the author

Sam James is a professional musician and amateur everything else from England. His writing's been featured almost nowhere—you can officially say you knew him before he went mainstream. Say you liked his blue period best, that'll impress the dinner guests.

Author's insights

'Would you believe me if I said I'd never heard the phrase "pick a winner" to refer to picking your nose until after I wrote this? I don't know whether I lucked out or accidentally did a "too literal" response to the prompt. Either way, I'm sorry!

'The concept of infinity has always fascinated me. This is not the first story I've written where an infinite supply of something is used as an energy source. It may not even be the grossest. We live finite existences in a finite world, and only really through fiction (and, more dryly, through maths) can we interact with truly endless amounts of snot. And that's beautiful to me.'

Ed's comments

Most people are aware of the more vulgar definition of 'picking a winner', but only one writer was bold enough to go knuckle-deep into the concept.

I didn't have 'wormhole up the nose' on my April 2024 *Not Quite Write Prize* bingo card, but here we are. Sometimes it's nice to take a break from all the dark and tragic stories and simply enjoy something truly absurd.

Amanda's comments

It's no secret I'm a big fan of stories that take a ridiculous concept and go hard. To me, this is where fiction shines – where the absurd can be our reality, even if only for a few moments.

But what really sold me was that this story went beyond its funny premise to deliver something deeper. In my mind, it offers a moment of hope in a world consumed by doom and gloom. Let's be real: we're all looking for a ray of sunshine to reassure us it's all going to be okay. This story offers just that.

Snot bad.

A GUIDE TO JUDGING THE PIE ENTRIES AT THE WOMEN'S AUXILIARY CLUB ANNUAL FAIR FROM LAST YEAR'S JUDGE WHO SHOULD HAVE KNOWN BETTER

Sally Simon

Look like you're taking notes. Lots of notes. Preferably in a small notebook that closes when you lay it down to pick up your fork, so that no one sees what you're really writing is a list of places you'd rather be, because let's face it, you already know which pie will come out on top and on whose chest you'll be pinning that oversized red, I mean blue, ribbon.

Unless someone has hit an entirely unpleasant menopause or her husband has been cheating on her, these will likely be the four top pies.

Mrs. Henderson's Blueberry Crumble

Nothing screams winner more than a brown sugar crumble over homegrown berries. Other women have tried, but this past champion has perfected the balance between sugar-coating and fruity goodness. If her tartness level is spot on, her pie will make you pucker.

Mrs. Murphy's Classic Apple

Some people think apple pie is boring. I say just because something is old and familiar doesn't mean it can't satisfy your taste buds. Trust me, you'll be pleasantly pleased.

Mrs. Humble's Gooseberry Pie

Don't make the joke. Not to her or anyone within earshot. It's not funny anymore. Seriously though. Have you ever tasted a gooseberry pie? Sometimes you don't know what you're missing until you know. Then, there's no going back.

Ms. Pryne's Strawberry Rhubarb

(the reigning champion)

Opposites attract. The long, tart vegetable meets its match coupled with the soft, sweet fruit we know and love. It's a risky combination. I used to be a fan, but everyone knows that already, don't they?

After your last bite, savor the moment. Sigh. Then lumber to the judges table, where you'll find a pitcher of water. Pour a glass and take a long swig. Try to not be overly dramatic. Hunch over your notebook while condensation builds on the glass.

Penelope Henderson, the past, present and future president of the Auxiliary will, at this point, nudge you and demand an update. 'How much longer could you possibly need?' she'll quip loudly before flirtatiously adding in a hushed tone, 'Your tongue must be so overly excited, with all that citrus.' She'll wink.

Make an effort to blow her off, enough for people to notice. 'He can't be bought.' That's what people will mutter and mumble amongst themselves.

Act like you're adding up numbers in your notebook. Scratch your head like it's long division.

I imagine there'll be quite a crowd this year. Last year, half of the contestants were on the other side of the midway watching a retired carnie bend himself into a pretzel when I proclaimed the winner. Not to worry, I'll be close at hand, sitting in the front row next to Penelope, (I've been forgiven). She'll squeeze my hand and whisper in my ear, 'He wouldn't, would he?'

I'll wonder too, but never admit it.

When a sizable puddle has formed below the glass, it's time to pick the winner. Stand. Ask yourself one last time if she's worth it.

Decide.

About the author

Sally Simon (ze/hir) lives in the Catskills of New York State. Hir writing has appeared in *Citron Review*, *Emerge Lit*, *Flash Flood*, and elsewhere. Hir debut novel, *Before We Move On*, released in Summer, 2024. When not writing, ze's either traveling the world or stabbing people with hir epee. Read more at sallysimonwriter.com.

Author's insights

'When I saw the "judging" prompt for the *Not Quite Write Prize*, the first thing I thought of was 4H, which is an agricultural-style organization in the USA. They hold summer fairs that host food contests, my favorite of which was pies. So, they were the obvious choice for me to base my story on. While attempting to come up with a unique format, I landed on trying a manual for the judge. But how could that be a story? That's when the main character, or POV manual writer, formed in my head.

'Set amongst the backdrop of small town, gossipy, rivalry, I used different types of pies to differentiate some of the women, and it ended up getting a bit juicy (pardon the pun). The manual turned more into a "read between the lines" cautionary treatise that left the reader wondering a bit. But I never was one for wrapping up my writing with a neat bow, or in this case, a blue ribbon.'

Ed's comments

Sally's story made me feel like Special Agent Fox Mulder, stapling pictures to the wall and connecting them with thumb tacks and coloured twine, trying to get to the bottom of who was behind this whole damn conspiracy.

I'm fairly certain that the narrator (the titular judge) is Penelope's husband, but what precisely transpired between him and the charming Ms. Pryne? And who is that strange man smoking a cigarette at the back of the room?

Amanda's comments

This was a standout for Ed from the get-go, but it was one that took its time (read: Ed's time) winning me over. Having said that, of all the bake-off entries that we received this round, this was the strongest.

What is immediately evident is that there is another story evolving just under the surface. I confess that I struggled at times to unpack exactly what was going on, yet it felt satisfying in the same way as an overheard conversation might – with enough snippets of juicy detail to keep me hooked.

Bake-off writers take note! This is how you deliver mouth-watering drama in fewer than 500 words.

HOT GIRL SUMMER

Laura J. Rayne

Sheri pulled over into the first parking lot she saw, tires crunching the broken pavement. Grabbing the crumpled brown paper, she pulled the dripping burger out of the bag before she had come to a full stop. The urge had itched at her for hours, even as she completed her food journal, ounces and calories meticulously recorded in perfect rows—red pen for fats, blue pen for carbs, green pen for fruits and vegetables.

There was never enough green pen.

'It's not your fault, Sheri.' They would mewl from their plastic-backed chairs, the condescending edge of their own victories cutting through the false staccato of their supportive words.

The grease from the burger dripped down her chin as she stared, eyes glazed and unfeeling, out the windshield at the dilapidated red bricks of the building.

'Just look at your food journal, hun.' The bottle-blonde would drawl as she pushed her fake tits so close that a person could do nothing but notice. They entered a conversation before she did, thrust into your field of vision by her exaggerated posture and pinched shoulder blades.

Seven weeks into the fitness challenge, and Sheri had yet to lose an ounce. They would pick a winner in just three weeks, and the thought gnawed at her. Falsifying the journal had become a compulsion that haunted her every moment. Her refusal to admit her shame to the self-righteous fakes was at odds with any genuine desire to change.

Shoving the last of the fries through salt-crusted lips, Sheri scrawled *Afternoon Snack: 2 ounces of almonds and fresh fruit* onto the open page on the dashboard and closed the worn, leather-bound notebook. Its gold-lettered enthusiasm glared back at her from the cover.

No food tastes as good as skinny feels.

Tearing her eyes away from the mantra, she crumpled the papered remnants of her afternoon snack and put the car in reverse, already calculating whether she would have enough time to throw up before her family got home.

About the author

Laura J. Rayne writes short stories that hit you right in the feels and bios that don't.

Author's insights

'Hot Girl Summer was born from the desire to explore the often unseen, yet immense, pressure society places on individuals—particularly women—to conform to certain beauty standards. The story delves into the emotional and psychological toll of these expectations, focusing on a character who battles with an eating disorder as she struggles to meet the idealized version of "perfection" that seems unattainable. Through her journey, I wanted to shine a light on the internal conflict of balancing self-worth with external judgment, and how that pressure can shape one's perception of themselves.'

Ed's comments

The experience of having our long term goals sabotaged by short term desires is certainly universal, and this story captures the resulting cognitive dissonance perfectly.

I loved the mature, intelligent and highly visual style that Laura chose to tell her story, presenting Sheri's actions truthfully and without moral judgement. If you are ever unsure of what is meant by 'Show, Don't Tell,' read this story.

Amanda's comments

This story sailed into the shortlist easier than most. What stood out to me was a strong emphasis on character. It's fair to say that very little happens, however we're left with a strong sense of the implications for our main character. There is subtext aplenty as we watch Sheri battle with her own reality.

A standout for me was the comedic line, 'They entered a conversation before she did, thrust into your field of vision by her exaggerated posture and pinched shoulder blades.'

Although this isn't a story to which I can closely relate, I do love a good carpark cheeseburger. In my circles, we call this a 'sneaky cheese,' and we enjoy it with no fucks given whatsoever.

5 stars.

ADVENTURE AWAITS

Terra Babcock

The human line snaked around the outside of the town hall and Ellie-May was smack dab in the middle of it with her momma. Normally Momma's strictness was speckled with smiles, but these past two days she'd been all rigid like a dead stick.

'Mitsy got picked last year.'

'Mmmhmmm.' Momma had thin lips that almost disappeared when she made that noise.

'I never get picked for nothing.' Ellie-May had won the talent show last spring, but that didn't count. She got that with work, and work wasn't lucky like the box.

'Let's hope it stays that way.'

'But Mitsy—'

'I don't want to hear another word about Mitsy.'

The talk always went like this with Momma. Even when she'd cried her eyes out because Mitsy never came back to tell Ellie-May about her adventures. She only knew the stories because her big brother Milton told her so at night while Momma was sleeping.

The lacquer box was so shiny it looked wet, with poppies and daisies brightly painted around the lip of the lid. The slot in the top was so thin she couldn't see inside. Paper slips and fountain pens sat in front of it.

Mr. Harper stood over the box and frowned when he saw her. His face had just about a thousand wrinkles, but she wasn't gonna count them all.

'Twelve already, girl?'

'Yessir.' She spread out her pale green skirt so he could see the careful embroidery around the hem.

'One slip.' He looked up at her momma. 'Two for you.'

Momma nodded curtly and wrote her name in careful cursive twice. Ellie-May's writing wasn't as pretty, but she'd worked hard at her letters, so her penmanship was the nicest in her whole class. It wasn't fair that all the grown-ups got two papers, and she only got one. They didn't even like adventures.

Ellie-May went to put her slip in the box, but her momma held up her hand. 'You really couldn't stop the children from entering? Not even after last year?'

'Town mandate, I'm afraid. Twelve and older.'

'You're the magistrate. You write the mandates.'

'And the people approve them.'

While they argued Ellie-May scribbled her name two more times and stacked them carefully under the first slip. There. Now she'd have three. Anyone who liked adventures deserved to have three.

'Fine.' Momma's last word was sharp but her hand shook.

Ellie-May slipped her papers in the box, careful to keep them in a neat little stack. Sneaking them in wasn't too hard since Momma looked away as if the beautiful box were a spider or a June bug.

They waited in the green in front of the town hall until everyone had their turn. Mr. Harper came out with the box and lifted the lid. His thick, old hands swirled the papers around before he pulled out a slip.

'Ellie-May.'

A hush like midnight swept over the crowd.

Ellie-May clapped, her smile as wide as her momma's eyes.

About the author

Terra Babcock is a writer, narrative designer, and game developer. She co-founded *Fiendish Fiction*, where she works with a small group to create visual novels that intertwine fiction with visual art and interactive branching narratives.

Author's insights

'When I was thinking over the prompt of "picking a winner" my mind kept wandering back to Shirley Jackson's *The Lottery*. The idea of using the same general concept but tackling it from the perspective of a child who saw the process of this sacrificial-type lottery as something positive that she wanted to win really stuck with me. I also wanted to use childlike observations in place of regular dialogue tags and keep the knowledge that something was wrong in town with the reader.'

Ed's comments

I loved the subtlety and craft of this piece: the way Ellie-May's innocent intentions and naïve interpretations, so perfectly captured in the close third-person perspective, propel us to a tragic conclusion our protagonist doesn't yet understand.

This kind of approach is extremely difficult to pull off effectively, and Terra has treated us to a masterclass.

Amanda's comments

This story had big *Hunger Games* energy. Above and beyond this idea was a deeply tragic sense of character, encapsulated by the paragraph, 'While they argued Ellie-May scribbled her name two more times and stacked them carefully under the first slip. There. Now she'd have three. Anyone who liked adventures deserved to have three.'

We're left desperately wishing Momma had been honest enough to spare this poor child from her unknowable fate!

Strong voice, evocative detail, and confidence in the reader's ability to read between the lines are what made this story a standout.

SURVIVAL GUIDE TO STAYING SINGLE

M. Lea Gray

'Radiant,' you agree. The bride glows under the spotlights in the center of the dancefloor, but you don't let yourself daydream about being her. You know, not everyone gets lucky. You know every girl lined up next to you thinks she deserves the next groom. Only one of you will survive catching the bouquet.

Blood runs down the bride's elbows and colours her creamy gown. Men block your way off the dancefloor.

'Ready, set—' a DJ mumbles into a microphone. One girl doesn't wait, and she jams her finger into another girl's eye. Wedding guests stomp, and you're sure the whole building will crash down and bury everyone alive.

The bride fakes the first few throws, but those of you with a plan hang back. You can't feel bad for the girls who fall first, not here, not now. As soon as they hit the floor, men grab onto their ankles and wrists—grab clumps of hair—and drag them into their new lives where their behaviour is corrected before they're dressed up for their first date and displayed like trophies.

It's you versus the bouquet, and when the bride pulls the ribbon loose, the groom's heart falls out of the center and rolls across the floor. No one moves to grab it because you all know you'll collide, hit the ground in pairs, get pulled apart, and tossed from man to man until there's nothing left of you but jagged bone.

You've seen women, know women who think they've prayed hard enough for a groom of their own. None of them survive the dancefloor. All of them are dragged away. It's to convince themselves because it doesn't convince you when you hear those women repeat, 'He's a good man.'

The bouquet goes high into the air and splits into wads of flesh, whole kidneys, and severed toes—pieces you don't recognize that the bride tore out of the groom with her bare hands. Teeth rain and scatter, so girls slip, and they're lost to the pack of men at the edge of the dancefloor.

Every move you make is life and death. When you see the groom's severed hand, you know you won't get another chance, so you dive for it. Ten women lost to one man kept is a ratio you refuse to accept. Behind your back, everyone whispers, 'She's difficult.'

The groom's bloody palm almost slips out of your grip, but you lace your fingers through it. You knew from the start, it's almost impossible to survive catching the bouquet. Even those men who'll take any woman still want to break her themselves, so as girls pile on top of you, claw at you for the groom's hand, you don't fight back. You don't even scream while they snap your arms and legs.

At least this way, you can put your pieces back together however you want instead of being forced into a shape you were never meant to be.

About the author

M. Lea Gray is a Canadian writer who loves trail running, watching movies, and eating (she really loves eating). More of her work can found in *Room Magazine*, *Fractured Lit Anthology 4*, and the Blue Cactus Press *If the Storm Clears* collection.

Author's insights

'Inspiration for *Survival Guide to Staying Single* came from my obsession surrounding antiquated gender roles and imagining the extremes women go through in different hellscape realities crafted by men. I tend to gravitate toward themes which examine the world we actually live in, not the world we pretend to live in, and even in the most dystopian nightmare, weddings/brides/bouquets would likely still hold steady as tradition.'

Ed's comments

M. Lea has a talent for highly creative and evocative premises. Her work feels like a sort of fugue-induced Jungian channelling of unconscious primal energies, rather than a premeditated piece of flash fiction.

Dripping with metaphor (and bodily fluids), her resulting commentary on dating and relationships resists precise analysis, but we can all certainly empathise with the intense feeling of urgency and frustration this grisly scene evokes.

Amanda's comments

After unpacking M. Lea Gray's most recent story as a January 2024 daredevil, I was pleasantly *un*surprised to find her latest effort on this round's shortlist.

What I loved most about this story was the taking of an innocuous and almost universally familiar scene and twisting it almost beyond recognition to say something new. The benefit here is that the scene is immediately familiar (requiring few words to explain) yet evocative in an exciting new way.

I will be stealing this flash fiction method for myself as soon as I can!

I remain convinced that with just the slightest bit more clarity around the messaging/intent behind this story, we would have crowned it number one. Thanks for the wild ride, M. Lea.

APRIL 2024 LONGLIST

The following list represents the remaining longlisted entries, in no particular order:

- **WILDCARD WINNER** – GRIEF by Leo Reese O Rinn
- **WILDCARD WINNER** – PICK ME by Linda Atkins
- THIRD TIME'S A CHARM by Kate Groth
- BYTE-SIZED by Arabella Peterson
- THE TEST by Steven Huff
- THE REMATCH by Monique Edwards
- TEN by Sarah Percival
- I WOULD ALWAYS CHOOSE YOU by Melanie Mulrooney
- TRIFECTA by Mathew Peters
- A DATE IN THE SAND by Frederick Dios
- THE CHOICE by Daniel Clark-Mudge
- FIRST ROUND KNOCKOUT by Jenna Treloar
- RHONDDA VALLEY, WALES, 1922 by Nick Smith
- THE ARRIVAL by Jo Skinner

- SALAD DAYS by Sarah Hurd
- APRIL RAIN by Kallie Poppleton
- AT THE 2011 COMPANY ANNUAL FUNDRAISER SOME THINGS NEED NOT BE SAID by Victoria Harris
- ATTRITION by Emily Rinkema
- HAPPY HOUR by A.J Blackman
- WORDS UNSPOKEN by Anna Volbrecht
- OUT OF THE RUNNING by Joel Woodard
- MAMA'S GIRL by Jennifer Quail
- BLUE, NOT PINK by Deidra Lovegren
- THE ABYSS by Aaron Wright
- THE INFINITELY GRATEFUL EX-MRS. CARL FISHER by Alex Atkins
- OREGON'S ANNUAL SEA GLASS SCAVENGER HUNT — IN COLLABORATION WITH SILETZ BAY GLASS BLOWING AND THE TOURIST BOARD OF LINCOLN CITY by Autumn Bettinger
- SPEAK NO EVIL by Jaime Gill
- HUSH by Sandra Kempen
- I'M NOT SORRY by Madeline Howard
- CLICKS, TICKS, TAPS, AND TIME by Samantha Ryan
- DOWN THE GARDEN PATH by Tess Allen
- **DISHONOURABLE MENTION** – READER DISCRETION ADVISED: COURSE LANGUAGE AND A STRONG SEX SCENE by Athena Law
- LATE FOR HIGH TIDE by Courtney Danielson
- FOR TWO STICKY BIRDS by Aeris Walker

Note: Since 2024, each judge has awarded a wildcard prize to an entry which did not make the shortlist but which we otherwise felt deserved recognition. We sometimes award a cheeky 'Dishonourable mention' to a story which raises our eyebrows in a manner only known to its author.

JULY
2024

Overview

The July 2024 *Not Quite Write Prize for Flash Fiction* challenged writers to create an original piece of fiction of no more than 500 words, which:

included the word **TABLE**.

included the action **'stealing something'**.

broke the writing rule **'avoid purple prose'**.

The competition drew **209 entries** from authors in **23 countries** around the world. That's **100,276** words for our judges, Ed and Amanda, to read. That's about the same number of words as ***The Hunger Games*** by **Suzanne Collins**.

Please enjoy the following top six stories from this round of the competition...

TWELVE JARS

Autumn Bettinger

There was always a soft beat, a gentle stirring. Lena opened pale eyes, long limbs curling under a mound of quilts. Rain pattered her window, and through the cracks crystallizing along the glass's edge, she could smell her garden. Thyme and rosemary, mint and mullein, all rose to twist along the droplets that splashed and shattered among the overgrown greenery.

As the beat grew louder, Lena unburied herself from her warmth. On the kitchen table, illuminated in the watery light of morning, sat eleven jars. In each, one living heart. Some palpated feebly, others pumped an anemic half-cadence.

'Shh, sweets.' She purred to the hearts as they *tha-dump, tha-dump, tha-dumped* hello.

Nibbling toast, her eyes trailed towards a counter where one jar remained. No more pulling hearts from the near-dead. The ones that couldn't fight back, the ones that smiled with relief as she cut those barely beating organs free. Today she would hunt closer to home.

Lena pushed the café's door open with a shiver of bells as the pretty little barista behind the counter waved.

'Lena! Look!' Sara thrust out her hand. An engagement ring gleamed, modest and delicate. The emptiness in Lena ached; she moaned softly.

'Are you alright?' Sara asked, thin eyebrows crinkling with concern. Lena waved her away.

'It's so gorgeous, it hurts!' She smiled—ignoring the density of loneliness that fell like gravity inside her—and ordered a latte.

'You know, I grow the most perfect blush-pink peonies,' Lena began. 'I actually have some cut stems in the car if you want to see? I'm happy to donate flowers for the wedding.'

'You'd do that?' Sara gasped, clutching her chest. Lena hungrily followed her hand. 'This coffee is on me, then! Meet you out back in ten?'

Sara fought, but Lena overpowered her with swift licks of her knife, ripping out that perfect, love-subsumed heart. Blood now soaked the interior of her Subaru. A ruby wash of intention.

Once home, Lena peeled off her clothes. The wound that ran from neck to navel was always slightly open, exposing the necrotic, gray interior of her cursed body. Her own missing heart had been sliced out by the practiced hands of a man who'd whispered *love, love, love.*

She had not been as cruel as him in her search for a replacement. She wouldn't keep them alive like he'd kept her. Like men had kept women for centuries: shells, left to rot.

Eleven hearts—pushing against their mason jars, all failed attempts that only lasted so long—beat hopefully as she took the latest, ineffectual heart from the grotesque cavity. It sputtered softly as she stroked it, beating a wheezing sonnet as it slid into jar twelve.

Sara's vascular offering squished in Lena's hand, viscous, pulsating. She pushed the cardiac promise inside her; a flush crept upwards as blood began to recirculate.

Stitching the wound closed, Lena smiled at her collection.

'Would you like to join your bodies in the garden?' she whispered and they all *tha-dump, tha-dump, tha-dumped* yes.

About the author

Autumn Bettinger is a short-form fiction writer and full-time mother of two living in Portland, Oregon. Along with winning the *Not Quite Write Prize*, Autumn has won the *Tadpole Press 100-Word Writing Contest*, the *Silver Scribes Prize*, has been shortlisted for both *Bridport* and *Bath*, and is the current 2024 *Fishtrap* fellow.

Author's insights

'The stealing prompt really spoke to my horror side, but the purple prose spoke to my enjoyment of lush language. Stealing literal hearts seemed like the perfect compromise. I have been having a love affair with women in gardens, writing about their lives in subtle, sinister ways. I wanted something melancholy, unsettling, but beautiful. These prompts really let me stretch my ideas without having to compromise on setting. I always love a woman with an ulterior motive, bonus points if she has a green thumb.'

Ed's comments

Our winning story was truly a standout, in what was a very strong round of competition.

Though its subject matter is rather grisly, *Twelve Jars* avoids the more vulgar payoffs of horror and shock value, opting instead to embrace surrealism and make it all about character.

Autumn's delicate, purplish prose presents us with a Lena who is as much hopeless romantic as she is cold-blooded killer, and whose grim actions feel somehow logical, even deserved.

Amanda's comments

This story was an easy pick for winner, with Ed and I quickly agreeing it should take the top spot.

By gradually revealing details supporting the premise, Autumn created a true reading *experience* for the reader to enjoy – taking us on a winding journey of discovery from start to finish.

What I loved most was how Autumn used the entire word count to maximum effect, weaving beautiful sensory details throughout (sights, smells and sounds), and creating an atmosphere in which the reader might immerse themselves. Favourites include the 'shiver of bells' and the masterfully repeated '*tha-dumps*' which round out the conclusion.

Christina Perri, eat your heart out! (No, not *literally*.)

IT'S HEADING FOR EARTH AND SPOILER ALERT: WE DON'T STAND A CHANCE

Dean Koorey

Professor Michelle Russo burst through the double doors of the government compound, a tangled mess of sweaty bangs, charts, laptops and dangling cables.

'I'm here to see General Brewster of the Planetary Defense Office,' she announced to the front desk clerk, her Jenga tower of items swaying precariously. 'He's expecting me.'

Russo, head astronomer at Murdoch Observatory, had been overseeing a routine scan of the night sky when she'd detected the rapidly approaching projectile. Now, fuelled by cold hard data and lukewarm coffee, she was here to brief the brass.

In the Situation Room, she spotted General Brewster immediately. A burly block of a man, he was as wide as he was tall. He occupied the far end of the table, flanked by an entourage of uniform-clad colleagues. Behind him, an enormous map of the world did its oscillating lines and digital clocks thing.

After quick introductions, it was down to business.

'Tell us what we're dealing with,' Brewster said.

Russo took a moment to check her charts and distribute the folders. She hadn't seen this much paperwork since her divorce. Take one, pass it on.

'Thank you General. At approximately oh-four-fifty this morning, my team detected a fast moving giant metaphor heading directly for Earth.'

A murmur broke out across the room, manila folders flopping open in unison.

Brewster eyed her amid the chaos.

'Did I hear correctly?' he asked. 'Did you say a giant *metaphor*?'

'That's right sir – we've never seen anything like it. Closest was the alliteration shower of '04 that famously flattened a frozen forest full of fifty-foot firs in Finland.'

Russo continued. 'However this metaphor is different. Its hyperbolic trajectory alone makes it bigger than anything else by a factor of infinity plus one.'

The room fell silent. Finally, Brewster spoke.

'Tell us straight, professor. How many lives are we talking?'

Russo consulted her notes. 'With this sized metaphor, we're predicting a torrent of ubiquitous pandemonium, spreading akimbo utilising a meandering miasma of maladies to serendipitously steal humanity's zeal, undeniably hastened and chastened by the certitude of our own requiem.'

The entourage exchanged glances. Russo sensed their uncertainty.

'I personally checked this data twice,' she reassured them.

Hands steepled, Brewster spun to take in the world map.

'And *where* is this giant metaphor expected to hit?' he asked.

'Based on its current course,' Russo began, 'destinations are but rusty map pins of the soul, akin to a paradoxical fool's errand in myriad emplacements amidst the loftiest latitudes of equanimity.'

'We have no contingency for that!' Brewster roared, fist firmly meeting table top. The room flinched.

'I'm recommending we initiate Code Purple,' he said at last.

'Professor, how long until impact?'

Russo punched some calculations into her laptop.

'Well, time is an ethereal gossamer thread, quintessentially measuring a plethora of perfumed petrichor memories effortlessly promulgating the ennui of a billion blazing Julys in the blink of an epoch's existence.'

She looked up from the data. The room stared blankly back.

'Basically, we're fucked,' she said.

About the author

Dean is a New Zealand-born, Australian-based, starry-eyed freelance copywriter who loves short stories so much that he co-created *Furious Fiction* in 2018 – probably inspiring *Not Quite Write* in the process. He has three freshly matured children and when not writing anthology-worthy pieces, you'll find him solving cryptic crosswords in his favourite café. Find out more at deankoorey.com.

Dean's work features twice in this anthology. You can find his other contribution at page 81.

Author's insights

'The "purple prose" anti-prompt led me to the "speaking in metaphors" definition and a link to "meteors". From there, it was only a short leap to my control room (a mash-up of *War Games* meets *Apollo 13*) and an *Armageddon/Deep Impact* plotline plus lots of nonsensical descriptions – which in hindsight probably could have been more flowery than pure silly. I'm proud of the picture I painted with this one though!'

Ed's comments

It's a simple little tweak – just replace 'meteor' with 'metaphor' – but in flash fiction that's all you need for a great story idea, and Dean has executed superbly.

In fact, he makes it look much easier than it is! All the elements of story construction have been tweaked to perfection. The action flows smoothly, and the pacing is perfect. And above all, it's highly entertaining from beginning to end.

Amanda's comments

This was a proper laugh-out-loud experience from a twice-shortlisted entrant (check out Dean's fourth place story from the January round on page 81). When I first read this story, I made a note of a favourite line, then quickly found I couldn't stop as it just kept getting funnier. It's the perfect example of just how far you can take the challenge of the anti-prompt if you let your imagination off the chain!

There are so many perfectly crafted moments, from the steepled hands to the divorce-like paperwork. (Although, I had to do vocal warmups to get me through that alliteration shower on the podcast...)

What was especially masterful was how Dean used the cliché 'situation room' setup we've seen so often in Hollywood as the framework to deliver original comedy – providing the perfect balance of serious and silly.

We determined this daring deed deserved dais distinction. Dazzlingly done, Dean!

BLURPLE

Roxanne Kubiak

My purple prince, my passion bringer, a towering fortress, the great pretender, I've watched you grow over many nights, as we've observed the liquid, glossy sun melt into the horizon and seen the moon dawn on us, I've held you tightly. You're so beautiful to me. Please, darling, don't let anyone tell you otherwise. I know you don't always see it, but I hope to be the mirror held up to you and when I do that, I see you two-fold and oh my god! I'm overcome by your handsomeness. Your poise, your strength, you're a beacon of hope that pulls me through the dark times. I wish I had the strength that you do, how do you cope with both the rough and the smooth and come out looking as you do? I just don't understand you, you're a jampot, an enigma, opaque and salaciously fruity.

When we're out together I find myself stealing looks at you, in the bathroom behind a blue door and I know that makes me uncouth. I'm sorry but with you, I just can't help myself.

I feel you reach depths I simply cannot, I look at you with pride and I understand you're a part of me and that pride should reflect back at me but in comparison, I'm awkward and unstable. My shoulders are stooped, slack and loose and my chin looks weak especially when I take photos from below. The shadows fall so heavily on my face and shame pulls it out of the frame entirely.

My chest it's just nothing to shout about, it isn't carved with those inexplicable, undecipherable, logographic six-packs. The ones I've seen on the movie screens, that are totally real and not just steroids and dehydration. I'm also short, there I've said it! I don't even hit six feet, I'm completely out of the running, but you, you surpass seven, I'm sure. I don't even need to measure you. I just need to look at you to know you're my best hope.

I took a photo of us, together and well honestly, it's all about you. I just pressed myself into the corner because being with you will make me look better. I hope you don't mind that I sent it to her. I need her to see what I see in you. If she replies 'Ewh, a dick pic'. King, I'll know she's not right for us.

About the author

Roxanne Kubiak is a fledgling writer hoping to survive the flight. She hails from the exotic and unknown city of Stoke-On-Trent, UK. Roxanne currently resides in Malaysia with her husband, (aka her ever suffering beta reader) and their two cats (backup beta readers). She is a woman of few words, except when talking, focusing primarily on microfiction and short stories. She enjoys raising caterpillars.

Author's insights

'Subconscious strands of inspiration were things like: a dick pic being the antithesis of how the female form is portrayed in traditional art via the male gaze, the manosphere and how it targets men with low self-esteem and how purple prose for me brings to mind romance, which I wanted to subvert (like Shakespeare's sonnet *My mistress' eyes are nothing like the sun*).

'However, the biggest inspiration was frustration. I'd struggled to shoehorn two other pieces to fit with the prompts, so I just wrote *Blurple* to amuse myself. I think if you can entertain yourself as a writer, you at least start with an audience of one.'

Ed's comments

I've spoken on the podcast about the pitfalls of twists that are not sufficiently supported by the story. Here is an example of a twist that worked extremely well, making me immediately re-read the story with a huge grin on my face.

What *Blurple* lacks in plot, it makes up for in voice and character. There's just something I find irresistibly amusing about the earnest and excessive manner in which our protagonist addresses his 'purple prince'.

But more than a just a comedic piece filled with double-entendres and dick jokes, what sets this story apart for me is the very real character that is being conveyed – one who is most definitely flawed, but also distinctive, fascinating, and surprisingly vulnerable.

Amanda's comments

When Poe uttered his famous *Single Effect* advice, I'm sure this story isn't what we had in mind, yet here we are! Every word of this story has been carefully chosen to support the final reveal.

On first read, this story delivers comedic shock value, and it only gets funnier from there as we realise how we've been duped by line such as, 'I don't even hit six feet, I'm completely out of the running, but you, you surpass seven, I'm sure.'

This story won Ed over, big time, and while I can't say I enjoyed it *quite* as much as he did, I will own that I found myself developing a strange sense of empathy for those poor, innocent souls who are simply trying to lead with their strengths in the dating market. A good villain origin story will do that to you.

PENNVILLE PARK

George Faville

Pennville twists like a pretzel. Its roads found new ways to bend after The Arrival in the park. Now the whole town folds in on itself like some massive origami middle finger to Einstein.

Our street was longer today. Uphill too.

Mel had stormed halfway down it before I reached her, panting.

'Please... wait a sec.'

'No.' Asshole.

Despite herself, Mel stopped next to the Reuter's fence, kicking a rock disdainfully into 'divinity'. Black ink wrapped every picket, shiny in the afternoon sun. Its sentences strangled the white paint, as the chalk beneath our feet did the pavement, as orange paint did each tree in town, as Dad's messy pen did the dining room table beneath Mel's yellow cover cloth.

If you want to know what's in the park, you'd only need to read.

'Where are you going?'

'I want to know what's in the park.' God, it was tempting to call her illiterate, but she already seemed so on edge.

'Ask literally anyone.'

'That wouldn't help, Nate.' She stomped on chalky 'salvation'.

'Then ask Dad!' I was stupid to remind her why she was mad. Mel started walking with renewed vigor.

'He'll just say the same empty shit he always does.'

'Mel, please, it's almost dinner. Who knows how long you'll be gone.' My racing heart stopped at the thought.

Mr. Grant had disappeared for almost a year.

'Haven't you read My Time Stolen?'

He'd written a book about it.

She scoffed. 'I could barely finish a page.'

It was dreadfully boring.

I paused atop a painted 'fool'.

The park was close today, we'd already reached its entrance. Mel didn't wait before charging in.

She'd be fine alone.

She'll be fine.

I ran after her.

Not a surface was clean from writing. No concrete visible beneath layers of words. No tree un-etched. Woodchips were dragged into paragraphs. I stomped through 'blinded', 'reify', and 'apotheosis'.

A crowd surrounded the swingset. Unmoving. Unspeaking. Unblinking. Staring solely towards its center. The only sound came from the rhythmic creaking of a rusty chain and Mel's shallow sobs. She repeatedly mouthed an inaudible something, terrified gaze fixed into the crowd.

A galaxy contained within transcendent skin danced with gravity atop the lonesome swing. Dawn broke atop its avatar. Stars whispered across its countenance. Nebulae formed, died, and burst within consecrated...

I didn't realize that Mel had grabbed my hand until she started sprinting away, dragging me with her.

'What did you see?' Her voice was raw and urgent.

'A galaxy contained within transcendent-'

'No. Tell me what you saw.'

'A galaxy contained- '

'Please Nate,' her voice cracked. 'Please. What was it?'

'Mel, I'm telling you. A galaxy- '

'One word Nate. It's one fucking word.' She was screaming, fear-stricken face wet with fresh tears. She started mouthing that inaudible something again. Over and over. Louder and louder in its silence. I shook my head, confused, and she crumpled to the pavement. Tears and snot and spit washing a 'bliss' away.

About the author

George is a college student currently studying Linguistics.

Author's insights

'I wanted to write something with Lovecraftian vibes because I thought it'd be an interesting take on the prompt: A cosmic horror so incomprehensible that we are forced to distance ourselves from its true nature through purple prose. It made for a fun write.'

Ed's comments

To paraphrase Winston Churchill (or perhaps Lisa Simpson), this story is like a riddle, wrapped in an enigma, wrapped in a scene from the movie *Inception*.

I loved the dreamlike elements of this story: the frantic searching through a shifting landscape, and encountering something powerful that is impossible to come to terms with.

I don't feel as though George has given us all the pieces we need to unlock this puzzle, but maybe that's why this story has stuck so persistently in our minds.

Amanda's comments

If you're anything like me, after reading this story, you might find your own brain has twisted like a pretzel, and you're no closer to an understanding of *what is on that damn swing*.

This story reminded me of the children's picture book, 'The Word Collector' by Peter H. Reynolds. It's a perfectly executed dip into the 'purple' words us writers and readers love, only ever adding value to the story rather than distracting from it.

What this story lacked in clarity it made up for in its clever take on the anti-prompt and its air of delicious mystery. As much as I would love to know what was on that swing (...Purple? ...God? ...Antidisestablishment-arianism?) I equally fear the knowledge might do me more harm than good.

A curiosity-provoking piece worthy of its place on the shortlist.

OFF ROAD

R. C. Barajas

How the birds got into the trailer, Dray couldn't imagine.

For the last 20 miles, he'd heard their rancorous caws from his place behind the wheel. Was it a murder of crows he was hauling across the desert? A murmuration of starlings? A deceit of lapwings…? An unkindness of ravens…

One moment his jeep was pulling an Airstream containing all his earthly possessions, swaying and veering as trailers do. The next, the trailer had lightened, levitating as hundreds of wings beat inside it, giving lift where there had been only drag. The ferocity of the beating wings came into a steady rhythm like so many oars stroking a Viking ship across the sapphire depths of a roiling sea.

Two sharp raps on his passenger window—something was gripping the door handle. A black pupil dilating in an amber orb was eying him imperiously, gray feathers vibrating with the uneven pavement.

Dray veered dangerously, but the trailer rose and compensated, the synchronized wings beating to level them smoothly back into a forward trajectory.

The creature rapped again. And Dray lowered the window.

First came the pointed head, the golden stiletto beak tucked back into the long neck which stretched suddenly forth, adder-like, upon rounded shoulders, feathers mottled as the sky before a storm. The imposing body followed, squeezing through the opening then falling with a thump onto the passenger seat, long knobbed legs in a scaly tangle, knocking Dray's coffee cup from the caddy.

'Pull this inelegant contraption to the perimeter, human!' cried the bird, fixing Dray in the crosshairs of its monocular gaze.

Dray cranked the wheel and hit the brakes, showering the road with loose gravel. Again the trailer lifted gently and alighted only when the jeep had come to a standstill on the lonely stretch of road.

The bird shuffled himself about on the seat until he balanced with haughty decorum. So tall was he that his neck coiled like the u-bend of a toilet, yet still the top of his tufted head brushed the ceiling.

'I am Indicus the Inimitable, Heron of Vengeance,' he cawed. 'My Siege of Brethren comes with a single purpose: to purloin! To decamp with your camper!'

He cocked his sleek head at Dray's confusion.

'We seek shelter from the destruction you and your kindred have unleashed. Our marshes and streams forever befouled, we shall use this structure as nursery for our chicks, hospital for our sick, and as a church where we may pray for your demise.' From the trailer came a unified thrumming of wings, the stamping of hundreds of scaly feet. Indicus blinked, and would have smirked, had the pointiness of his beak allowed it.

'Unhook the tethered carriage, human!' And fast as a fish, Indicus held his razored beak to Dray's throat.

In the empty stretch of road littered with his possessions, Dray watched as his Airstream, now filled with a Siege of Herons, Indicus the Inimitable at the fore, lifted and took gracefully to the sky.

About the author

R. C. Barajas is surprised by most things. An artist and writer, she is a Californian by birth and a Virginian by transplant.

You can virtually pay her a visit at rcbarajas.com

Author's insights

'This all fell together with the prompts. "Table" found itself inside Inimitable, and The Great Heron was named after one of our dog Indie's nicknames: Indicus. Herons, if they spoke, would certainly use purple prose – I mean, just look at them. And as for the act of stealing, what birds of any feather wouldn't want to take an Airstream from a planet-befouling human?'

Ed's comments

This one is all about atmosphere. R.C.'s rhythmic, lightly purple prose lends a cinematic air to this unusual little scene, making it feel like something out of a twisted *Breaking Bad* cold-open.

The surreal events that unfold come as a surprise, and I've found that surprising the judges often goes halfway towards impressing us.

Amanda's comments

This story is a great example of how far brainstorming the prompts can take you. In this case, R. C. has taken the collective noun of a 'siege of herons' in response to the 'stealing something' action prompt and run it to its extreme, delivering a whacky, original creation.

I enjoyed R.C.'s beautiful imagery, such as the Viking ship's stroking oars and the coiling neck of Indicus, each line bringing the story to life in my mind and rendering the absurd real.

I have to confess that the talking bird halfway through the story came as a jack-knife in tone for me, and I would have loved to have seen this story told as a straighter Hitchcockian thriller. Having said that, using the bird as the purple orator was a wise move, and overall, the original premise and masterful scene-setting are what earned this story its place on the shortlist.

THE EASTER BUNNY IS COMING!

Tabbie Hunt

Oh, shit! I've eaten Easter. It's midnight, the shops are closed, and my kids are expecting chocolatey enchantments in approximately six hours. Oh god, I've stolen their happiness. I wish the bloody Easter Bunny was real.

'Quelle surprise!' sighs my cat.

I stare at the ground.

'Well, there remains but one choice,' he says, and without further ado, he extends a claw and slices through the very fabric of my kitchen universe.

'What the—'

'Oh, settle yourself. If you can conceive of my supernatural speech, then this lies within the bounds of your brain!' says my cat. 'Now, in you go!'

'You're not coming?' I ask.

'I'm not the one who has been wayward!'

He gives me a shove and I'm suddenly somewhere else entirely: a damp, earthy-smelling tunnel, carved out of warm, yellowy-brown rock. A line of people stretches ahead of me. Some are silent, some are crying quietly. A pinched-looking woman in front of me turns round.

'Did you steal their eggs too?'

Before I can answer, an impossibly large rabbit appears beside us.

'Silence!' he snaps.

We comply.

After two maybe three hours of slowly shuffling forward – god I'm thirsty and I really need a wee – I catch sight of a large, circular wooden door. People go in, one at a time. They don't come out. Fuck!

An hour or so later, it's my turn. I'm visibly trembling as I step through the doorway. Inside is a burrow, sparsely furnished but nonetheless cosy. A handsomely formidable rabbit stands before a roaring fire.

'You're not—'

'I am,' he sighs. 'Forced into existence once a year by a sharp increase in belief.'

'Ah, the children—'

'No, it's you lot! Pathetic parental porkers and their last resort desperation. Every. Single. Time!'

'I'm sorry, I—'

'Let's get to it! What'll you give me for the eggs?'

'Er, what do you want?'

The Easter Bunny takes my hands, pulling me towards him, then one paw pushes me down until my legs fold and my head is level with his groin. You've got to be fucking kidding me...

Sometime later, I find myself back in the kitchen, just as sunrise smiles at the window. I fling myself through the back door.

Delightful, frosted bunny prints lead up the path and across the lawn. The entire garden is twinkling with the most gorgeous chocolate jewels and there is a basket of cheeping chocolate chicks on the picnic table. It's beyond magical.

'Is that chocolate riming your mouth?' my cat titters.

'You knew? You piece of—'

'Obviously,' says my cat, 'but on the off chance that you deigned not to swallow your...er...pride, I procured replacements, weeks ago.' He waves a plastic bag bulging with eggs.

'You set me up...why?'

'You will recall the occasion you placed a cucumber at my rear because TikTok decreed that I would believe it was a serpent. And your unwarranted cackling when I screamed. Well, you may now consider us even, bunny blower!'

About the author

Tabbie Hunt is a children's book-packager turned freelancer, who writes in the small cracks between life. She is particularly interested in failings, feelings, and funniness and her work can be found online and in various anthologies.

Author's insights

'This story was born when a TikTok video about cats and cucumbers collided with a hidden packet of Easter eggs. As I sat there with chocolate around my mouth, I started to think about suitable punishments for such a heinous crime, what bunnies do best and, well, you know the rest!'

Ed's comments

Stealing our kids' chocolate right before Easter is an annual tradition in my household – but that's where the similarities to this story end!

I applaud Tabbie's willingness to go weird with this one. It takes a certain amount of courage to suppress that inner voice that is always trying to get us to self-censor and take a more traditional route. While the traditional approach feels safer, unleashing your id on an unsuspecting public is where the real fun is!

Amanda's comments

Jaw, meet floor.

When I started reading this story, I chuckled along with the relatability of a parent stealing a child's Easter eggs (guilty!) The story very quickly threw me off kilter with a talking cat and space-time continuum tear. Little was I or any other reader to know that this would be the least of my worries!

I loved this story for its comedic shock value and clever moments, such as the Easter Bunny being forced into existence each year by a sharp increase in belief... not from the children, but from those chocolate-stealing parents!

Given the prompts this round, I also find it particularly apt that Tabbie's story should *steal* the Honourable Mention position from the grasp of past winner, Athena Law.

It's a story I'm sure Athena *and* I will never forget...

JULY 2024 LONGLIST

The following list represents the remaining longlisted entries, in no particular order:

- **WILDCARD WINNER** – FRIDGERTON – A LOVE STORY by Athena Law
- KINGDOM OF THE UNHOUSED by Martini Lynne
- SOOTHSAYER by Kavya K
- PASS THE SALT by Chloe Hor
- ON THE VERANDA OF A CABANA NEAR HAVANA by Craig Goddard
- THE COLANDER by Valentine O'Connor
- WHY I'M SINGLE by Jen Fortner
- FOR BLIND DATES, WE WEAR PURPLE by BL Phillips
- YOU WEREN'T JUST BORN by Jasmine Johnstone
- TIME THIEF by Natalie Harris
- AFTER A SEX DREAM ABOUT MY BROTHER, I RETHINK EVERYTHING, STARTING WITH TEQUILA by Emily Rinkema
- LOST AND FOUND by Nikki Crutchley

- MARINATED GOATS' BALLS by Anne Moorhouse
- BUT ONE MAN LOVED THE PILGRIM SOUL IN YOU by Linda Atkins
- THAT WHICH IS TAKEN by Púca Beag
- HOT DESKING by Lucy Mac
- WHOSE GOD IS IT? by Teegan Thornhill
- A GOLDEN POCKET WATCH by Madeline Howard
- PUTTING AFFAIRS IN ORDER by Jo Skinner
- THE DEVIL'S TABLE by Rebecca Ahola
- INSURMOUNTABLE by Christina Wilson
- A PURPLE PULSE THAT BEATS THROUGH TIME by Melanie Mulrooney
- NOTEWORTHY by Holly Brandon
- PEARL'S FAILURE TO WRITE A SONG IS IN NO WAY MY FAULT by Romany Jane
- VALERIE (OR, THE VIXEN WHO HAS STOOD AS BOTH MY CLOSEST CONFIDANTE AND ONGOING ADVERSARY SINCE OUR TENDER DAYS OF YOUTH, OUR PERPETUAL RIVALRY THE HARBINGER OF MY EVENTUAL DOWNFALL) by Sheridan Bell
- THE DATE by Amanda Larson
- LET GO by Lauren Dougherty
- LILAC'S PROTECTION by Morgan West
- HIS PURPLE REIGN by Jaime Gill
- THIS IS WHY WE CAN'T HAVE NICE THINGS by Sanya Dimova
- THE KINDNESS OF STRANGERS by Elaine Joy Degale

- GOOD FIRST IMPRESSION by Rachael Crane
- HONEYED VOICE LIKE A SONG by Chloee Thornhill
- TILL DEATH DO US PART by Kaylie Smith

The following story did not make the longlist but received a wildcard prize:

- **WILDCARD WINNER** – DEMOCRACY MANIFEST by Eunice Armitage

Note: Since 2024, each judge has awarded a wildcard prize to an entry which did not make the shortlist but which we otherwise felt deserved recognition.

OCTOBER 2024

Overview

The October 2024 *Not Quite Write Prize for Flash Fiction* challenged writers to create an original piece of fiction of no more than 500 words, which:

included the word **PALM**.

included the action **'telling a lie'**.

broke the writing rule **'avoid head-hopping'**.

The competition drew **184** entries from authors in **15** countries around the world. That's **87,776** words for our judges, Ed and Amanda, to read. That's about the same number of words as *1984* **by George Orwell**.

Please enjoy the following top six stories from this round of the competition…

I TOLD YOU THIS WAS A POEM

Taurenelle

I told you this was a poem
when you asked why I was crying.

You sat on my lap,
counting the syllables on your fingers,
hoping to keep its rhythm with your palms.

You'll read this again
when you're older,
searching for a reason and finding no rhyme.

I told your mother this was a memoir,
but she didn't know I was starting with the end.

Amanda was in the kitchen. Chopping and stirring and waiting
for it all to bubble to the surface. She knew Isaac was taking it

hard. He was the strong, silent type, growing less strong and more silent as the months went by. Now, he was weak and mute and refusing to move on.

The blade nicked the inside of her thumb. She bled onto the counter and on the carrots and all over her favorite apron. She quickly cleaned it up and got on with making dinner. That's what she did. She got on with things.

'A quarter less but a tenth as joyful,' she mumbled to herself. Contemplating the strange recipe of a shattered home.

'Is that from one of your poems?' Kayla asked, hoisting her little body onto a stool and stealing a piece of celery.

Amanda hadn't written in nearly a year. Not for lack of emotion. Perhaps for the opposite. 'Umm. Yes, dear.'

'Does it rhyme?' Kayla preferred limericks; her brother had liked haikus.

'I'm afraid not.'

'Then I don't want to hear it.' Kayla was growing sick of the sadness. What's the fun of having writers as parents if they only write boring stuff? Her mother used to tell stories about basilisks and gnomes and castles under volcanoes. She even named one of the faeries Kayla. And Alex was the boy who lived forever. Now, she only turns the light off and says goodnight. Even the wishing of tight sleeps and the warding off of bed bugs were a thing of the past.

'Not everything is fun all the time. How have you not learned that yet? After everything? You're almost eight years old, for Christ's sake.' It was as if someone else had yelled at her daughter. Perhaps *she* was someone else. Or perhaps she wasn't anyone at all. Whoever she was, she took a deep breath and got on with things. That's what she did. She got on with things while Isaac sulked in his study.

I told your mother it was for safety,
and kept it with the deed and the will and my grandfather's watch.

The year Longfellow published Evangeline.
I should have known he'd know.

I'd like to think this is poetic.
That what I'm about to do...
rhymes.

Maybe an elegiac couplet:
the father having six feet;
the son having five and a half.

Or maybe it's just an elegy.
Or maybe I'm just a fool.

I told you this was a poem
when you asked why I was crying.

But I think you knew it wasn't.
It's just a reason without a rhyme.

About the author

If Taurenelle had to describe himself in three words, they would probably be: unparalleled genius, devilishly handsome, humble, and terrible at counting. He is a trained classicist, an occasional poet, and a budding comedic fantasy author who only speaks in the third person. He resides in New York City, where he finds endless ways to distract himself from writing (or being a productive member of society in general). He is currently falling in love with the art of flash fiction thanks to *Not Quite Write* and – since he just learned what a chapbook was yesterday – is hoping to publish one within the next year.

Author's insights

'Of the three writing prompts, I first gravitated to "telling a lie." I knew I wanted to write something that, in and of itself, was a lie, and being a lover of poetry, the first thing that came to me was the line, "I told you this was a poem." Almost instinctively, it was followed by "when you asked why I was crying." From there, I had to discover who this character was, why he was crying, who he was lying to, and ultimately, why he was using poetry to do so.

'Moreover, I wanted the reader to struggle to define what they were reading. Some of it is formatted like a poem, but there is no meter or rhythm to the verses, and the prose portion uses poetic language and almost has a melody of its own. So, what is going on here? I told you this was a poem, but is it?

'When I had to incorporate the "head-hopping" prompt, I knew I wanted to use different perspectives to give the reader new pieces of information that slowly unveiled the story.

'I didn't want to end the piece with a punch, as most flash fiction tends to do, but softly and sweetly, and perhaps requiring a second read to get the big picture. But mostly, I wanted to write something pretty.'

Note: This story was resubmitted with edits for this anthology.

Ed's comments

This story floored me.

Each element converges towards a single effect. References to 'rhyme and reason' not only encapsulate the family's search for understanding that is its primary theme, but this motif also extends to the structure of the story itself – poetry and prose – a structure which in turn reinforces the split-perspective narration, with 'rhyme' and 'reason' each reflecting the different way in which Amanda and Isaac deal with their loss.

The reveal is handled with incredible subtlety, but there are enough clues for the reader to piece together this deeply multilayered and tragic story.

Amanda's comments

Once again, we've been foiled by a poet.

The word that first springs to mind is 'layers'. While I marked this as a favourite from the very first read, it only grew on me once I peeled away those layers to discover the hidden gems within.

On its surface, it's a melancholic story about a man (and family) in crisis, but it is the artful use of subtext which delivers more on each careful read.

There's the 'story within the story' of parents who have lost a child and how they are each processing their grief. There's the story of a daughter, full of childlike hope against all odds. And there's the story of the power of the written word, and how a line like, 'the year Longfellow published Evangeline,' can send the uninformed among us (me) down a search engine rabbit hole so deep that we (I) emerge, sometime later, crying.

The lie, which forms the framework for this story, is simultaneously simple and complex, and the head-hopping, while jarring, offers a window through which readers might imagine the story that comes after 'The End.'

NINE TIMES SEVEN IS SIXTY-THREE

Emily Rinkema

They know the drill, have done it almost monthly since starting school, but this is different. Ms Callahan's voice is sharp when she tells them to move to the back of the room—now—under the whiteboard with Luke's scrawled complex sentence example. He wishes he hadn't used the name Tommy in his sentence because maybe it's obvious that he likes him, that he's written the name in his notebook hundreds of times. When they hear the *pop pop pop*, Kelly thinks she's not going to fall for it this time, not like last time when she hid behind the historical fiction shelf in the library because there was a shooter, only it wasn't a shooter, it was the community service club doing a balloon popping fundraiser, and everyone laughed at her, except Siobhan, who apologized when no one was looking, who recognized herself in Kelly, someone who was quick to hide, quick to stay out of the way of loud noises and breaking dishes and open palms. Balloons, Kelly thinks, just balloons, and Kevin breathes in through his nose, out through his mouth, just like his mom taught him, just like they practiced at home, and he does his times tables in his head, also his mom's suggestion, because numbers make sense to him, unlike people and words, and he's on threes now–three times four is twelve, three times five is fifteen, three times six is eighteen–and *pop pop pop*, only louder, and Ms Callahan–Andrea–tries to picture her daughter, who is in art class in the blue wing right now, but she can't remember what she was wearing when she ran out of the house this morning, and it's so important that she remember, that she can bring up an accurate picture of her. Cameron taps his index finger on the floor next to Luke's sneaker, tap, taptap, tap, tap, tap. He's tapping out a song he's singing in next week's holiday concert, only he keeps messing it up, and he knows his dad will notice and will tell him he has to work harder if he wants to be someone, if he wants to matter– and six times four is twenty four and six times five is thirty and six times– *pop pop pop pop* –and Davis flinches, leans into Andrea, grabs her hand, and she whispers to him, to them, to herself, 'We're going to be okay. I promise, we're going to be okay,' and eight times six is forty-eight and eight times seven is fifty-six and eight times eight is sixty-four and it wasn't the blue sweater, it was the green jacket, the one they bought her for her fifteenth birthday because she had asked for it, because she said it would make her so happy, and if Luke gets out of here he will tell Tommy, and yes, it was the green jacket, she's pretty sure, and did she yell after her? Balloons, just balloons. Did she tell her to have a good day? She thinks so.

About the author

Emily Rinkema is not working on a novel. While not working on a novel, she's usually writing flash, sometimes eating Ring Dings and watching British crime dramas, too often imagining how much better sleep would be if arms were removable, and always avoiding sinkholes. Follow her on X, BS, or IG at @emilyrinkema or read her work at emilyrinkema.wixsite.com/my-site.

Author's insights

'The head-hopping prompt threw me for sure. I had a dozen false starts, but when I landed in a classroom, a place I've spent more hours than anywhere else in my life, I knew I had the right setting. As an educator in the US, I spend way too much time imagining what I'd do in a school shooting. I know what it's like to be crouched in the classroom when a drill is called, everyone alone with their thoughts and fears–so I imagined the range of those thoughts and the strategies we all develop to live in our heads when we're terrified.'

Ed's comments

Stream-of-consciousness is a perfect response to this round's anti-prompt, and Emily has executed this style with subtle precision. The hop from one character's perspective to the next feels smooth and entirely natural, and the frenetic narration elevates the tense mood of this scene.

But what I find most impressive is how, through a string of carefully selected details, she manages to rapidly convey and develop half-a-dozen distinct characters. Moments like Ms Callahan dropping her title – signalling her powerlessness in that moment – help to ramp up the drama as the story drives towards its inevitable conclusion.

The choice to end the story before the anticipated moment ensures that the tension lingers on in the reader's mind. This is truly a story that stays with you.

Amanda's comments

When I first read this story, I commented that it gave me 'literal chills.' This wasn't some kind of elder millennial hyperbole, I did in fact experience a physical reaction similar to goosebumps after reading this story, not just the first time, but on each repeated reading. I have them again now.

The subject matter is grim, but somehow, Emily has found the beauty in it, and the result is a master class in character. We spend only a fleeting moment with each of these characters however, much like time might slow down preceding the moment of impact in a car crash, each fleeting moment here expands to suggest a whole life, giving us enough to form that crucial emotional connection and investment.

The single head-hopping paragraph builds breathless momentum as the story progresses, with the device of the times tables functioning as its ticking clock. The careful choice of first line combined with the cinematic 'cut to black' at the end gives us the opportunity to wonder, and guess, at the horrific implication of that title.

THE TIP OF THE TONGUE THE TEETH THE LIPS

Eilish Forwells

You've heard what they say about the salesman who trades in voices. You know he can't be trusted, but at the chime of your bell, you creak open the door and usher him in. You crack him a smile, you tell him to sit, you serve hot tea and some shortbread and let him begin.

'Palmer J. Calliope's the name, trading voices is my game,' he says between bites.

You raise your eyebrows in mock surprise. 'I didn't know you could do that,' you lie. Your voice is brittle, like an aged tree collapsing in the howling wet winds of a winter.

'It's simple, really.' He pauses, slurping his tea and preparing his pitch. 'For a reasonable price, you can transform your voice into that of another—for a night, a lifetime, or even just an hour. I've got seven types of laughter. Perhaps a snort or a chuckle? Or something sultry and smooth? Or haunting, like a poet? Escape for a while—distract from your worries and lighten your woes.'

But the so-called 'vocal exchange' is no secret to you. He thumps his case on your table and snaps open the clasps. Melancholic whispers seep out as he raises the lid, he reveals rows of chattering vials that quiver and clink.

'Purchase a vial, and the voice is yours—at least for a while. Trust me, it's worth it.' He smiles, raising his palms as if baring his soul.

Your hand trembles as you scan the labels. It must be in there.

'What if I wanted,' you ask, 'a mellifluous voice?'

'Ahh,' he murmurs. 'There is only one that would do. Pricey but the real deal, you would sing like an angel.' He pulls out a small vial with a cool purple hue. 'Here. Take a listen.'

For a moment, there's silence. You lean in, holding your breath. Straining, you can hear the faintest of singing—beautiful rich flaming notes that nourish your heart. A melody from a lifetime ago.

You'd heard your voice once before, singing on a stage—in the mouth of a performer who boasted of fortune and glorious fame. You captured her, and blotted her with blood, you stole the tip of her tongue, and she gave you his name: Calliope the salesman, the trickster, the villain.

You check your watch. It must be about time, poison hemlock works quick.

His mind is sluggish, like it's wrapped in treacle, he can't help but think, has he seen you before? He remembers the girl whose mother sold him a voice, it was the deal of a lifetime, a steal at that price.

You stare as his body slumps heavy in his chair. Death will devour him and flee with his soul. Your smile drips with venom and without hesitation, you snatch up the vial and swallow the contents whole.

I am complete once again. I am one with my mellifluous voice, and once more I can sing with the sweet innocence of summer and spring.

About the author

I'm a completely amateur writer living in Scotland with my wife and dogs. When I am not working or writing you'll probably find me swimming in a loch or drinking whisky.

Author's insights

'The idea was originally inspired by a weekly writing challenge to create a micro story titled *Whispers in the Dark*. I had a very clear image of trapped voices in a dusty old brown suitcase wanting to get free. It was half baked, and I couldn't stop thinking about it. The *Not Quite Write Prize* offered me the opportunity to bring this story to life. I loved the thought of voices moving between people and using someone else's voice as a form of escapism, it felt to me like an addiction, a way to hide from everything that didn't feel quite right.'

Ed's comments

This entry is a *story* in the true sense of the word. We are taken on a journey that spans a lifetime, culminating in a satisfying and earned moment of revenge. Eilish weaves the backstory inconspicuously into the action, which remains dynamic and rooted in the present.

What impressed me most about this story is the way in which the setting is so effectively evoked. I can picture the room and the characters clearly in my mind, yet there is very little physical description!

Amanda's comments

This story was an instant favourite of mine from the first read, and landed easily on the shortlist as the first contender Ed and I agreed on.

Eilish's choice of intriguing title and second person POV, use of vivid imagery ('rows of chattering vials that quiver and clink'), and masterful execution of voice combine to fully immerse the reader into the scene.

What I loved most about this story was the strong sense of cohesion, with auditory details throughout supporting the story's central premise.

I feel a stronger ending could have seen this story rise to first place, which just goes to show that the writing 'rules' do exist for a reason. Nevertheless, I applaud Eilish's embracing of what was a very challenging anti-prompt.

LOVE STRUCK BY A LAMPPOST

J. Lewis-Edney

Sandra knew what she wanted in a man: tall, dependable, bright, and most importantly, someone who didn't answer back.

The guys tonight had been dead weight—a who's who of who's not. Raggedy, rude, and relentless in their pursuits. She hated a try hard.

The sun was beginning to rise as she stumbled down the pavement, an unfortunate smell of alcohol induced vomit still clinging to her skin-coloured tights.

Most of the lampposts had turned off their lights for the sunrise, all except one. She stopped as she passed it.

In her drunken stupor, she looked up at the light.

'See, you're what I'm looking for, sweetheart,' the last word was particularly slurred. She reached out and grabbed the lamppost with a clammy palm and began twirling around. 'You wouldn't disappoint me, staying alight while all the others just give up so easily,' she said as she spun.

The lamppost did not respond; he also did not know why he was still on when all his brethren were asleep. Probably a wiring issue.

'I'm Sandra, twenty-eight,' the forty-year-old said. 'An Aries, so fiery in the streets and commanding in the sheets, if you know what I mean!'

The lamppost stood stoic. He did not know what she meant; he had no concept of star signs.

'I tried that line on some of the guys tonight, you know? Set expectations and all.' Sandra swayed on her feet. 'But the ones interested weren't exactly Ryan Reynolds.' She huffed, standing right in front of the lamppost now, chin tilted up.

The lamppost was not familiar with Ryan Reynolds; maybe he was another like him, filled with steel-wired cabling and a low-pressure sodium lamp.

Sandra's head wobbled as her gaze travelled up and down the lamppost's simple, sleek form, tracing its curves as her eyes roved. 'Solid, reliable,' she muttered. One hand still clung to the metal, and she pressed her cheek against its cool surface. 'You're so strong.'

In the sticky summer heat, the lamppost's chill soothed her flushed face. Her hands slid lower, gripping him tighter. She sighed, imagining what it would be like to kiss him.

The lamppost could only watch on as she leant forward, her lips in a strange contortion as she went to press them against his base.

Thud.

Before her lips could make contact, her forehead beat her to it, the sound echoing down the street.

'Holy fuck,' she shouted, recoiling in pain.

'What the hell am I doing!' she screamed, desperately rubbing her forehead.

She balled her fist and took a swing at the lamppost, completely missing and falling flat on her face. She was splayed on the ground, her cheeks red, eyes wet and wondering how this was her life.

As Sandra lay there, defeated, the light above her flickered once. And then, with a soft click, it went out.

About the author

Jack Lewis-Edney is a project manager from the south of England, now living in Australia. He writes contemporary fiction focused on the humour of everyday situations. When not tapping away at his keyboard you'll find him playing video games, crocheting, or playing fetch with his fluffy Tibetan Spaniel.

Author's insights

'The anti-prompt is really what fuelled my inspiration here. I thought it would be fun to explore two extreme perspectives. After one or two Friday night drinks, I know all too well how ridiculous a drunk person can be. So, what's the complete opposite of that? My bright idea (sorry), was a lamppost. Sometimes you want to read something deep and insightful, and sometimes the best stories are downright silly. I definitely leant into the latter with this one. Surprisingly, giving personality to an inanimate object came far easier to me than crafting one for a person. Maybe there's some deep dive into the human psyche waiting to happen there—or maybe I just relate more to a lamppost.'

Ed's comments

We've all been there.

Even those who can't relate directly to operating under extreme levels of intoxication will surely find something universal in this humorous tale of frustrated soul mate searching. We've certainly all been *there*.

This was such a unique and surprising take on the anti-prompt, with the lamppost's views on astrology elevating the absurdity of this romantic little scene.

Amanda's comments

I fought for this story. It was a favourite from the get-go, almost certainly because it ventured into the 'inanimate object romance' genre I have so recently come to adore.

It's challenging to deliver slapstick comedy in a non-visual medium, but Jack pulls it off with flair. Lines like, 'The lamppost was not familiar with Ryan Reynolds,' and 'He had no concept of star signs,' position the lamppost as the (literal) 'straight guy' for our inebriated protagonist's 'funny guy'.

Much like the quintessential tragic clown, however, there's an underlying sense of sadness peeking out from behind that mask. As humans, we all know what it's like to feel lonely, and I couldn't help but feel a pang of empathy for Sandra after that closing line.

So, while it's undoubtedly a fun story, it's that delicate walking of the line between light and shade – that poignancy – which, to me, truly set it apart.

SHARPENED STAKES

Sheridan Bell

I'm no gambler, but I'm always making bets with myself.

Okay, Sienna– hold your breath for forty seconds and you'll make the squad.

Some people use clairvoyants to gain a sense of control over their lives. Me? I strike deals with God.

Don't eat the last biscuit and when you wake up tomorrow that zit'll be gone.

Mind you, if I believed in God, I'd just ask Her directly.

Finish your essay by 8pm and tonight he'll call.

At 7.57pm I type the final word. My cellphone buzzes.

Entering the diner, the air is hot, thick, and heavy with the smell of burnt grease, and indifference. I scan the room and, for a split second, think the slight, bearded man in a plaid shirt at the bar might be him. Then the real thing waves to me across the room – clean-shaven and sharp-featured like a young James Bond, or an old Peter Parker.

'Hey, kiddo,' he says, pulling me in for a hug. The scent of sunscreen and tobacco takes me back to the beach when I was eight and he was still my whole world.

'Hi, Dad.'

He holds me a second too long. I pull away and slide into the booth. The cracked red leather–sticky with spilt soda and residual body heat – slaps my thighs.

'I ordered you a pink panther. That still your favourite?'

'Sure.'

He asks how school is going. I fabricate my sporting successes, exaggerate the size of my friend group, until our drinks arrive.

If the next song is from the eighties, you'll apologise for taking so long to call.

The viscous liquid slides down my throat like half-frozen jelly with a sickly-sweet raspberry-bubblegum aftertaste.

You'll promise to see me more often.

An inefficient fan whirrs above us, dispersing humidity about the room.

And you'll mean it.

'You said you have good news...' I prompt.

He clears his throat and takes a swig of beer. Even the bottle is sweating. In the background, TLC trills about chasing waterfalls.

'I've been promoted.'

'Congrats.'

He raises his arm to wipe his brow, revealing the darkened stain of his underarm.

'Miranda and I are moving to Queensland.'

If that guy makes eye contact, you'll choke on your Heineken.

Plaid-shirt man glances up. I quickly look away.

My father claps his palms together in a prayer position, then lets them fall, pointing towards my crossed arms.

'So...what do you think?'

If I tell the truth, you'll surprise me.

'Well, that sucks.'

He nods and leans back, studying me with keen eyes. He's thinking my hair's dirty, I've gained weight, and lost confidence – he's ashamed of me.

'You look more like your mother than ever.'

I slump further in my seat, clammy thighs slipping over the distressed fabric.

If I don't cry, you'll stay.

'Hey, Sienna – it's a compliment. She was gorgeous when we first met.'

I look at him and a single tear escapes.

So I'm right, but there's no joy in my victory. Next time, I'll up the ante.

About the author

Sheridan Bell is a school teacher, who lives in New Zealand with her husband and son. Writing is one of her favourite things to do, and she has enjoyed making up poems, stories, and plays to entertain friends and family since before she could hold a pencil.

Author's insights

'"Making bets with myself" is something I have done for as long as I can remember (surely, I'm not the only one?), and I have been waiting a while to include this quirk in one of my stories. When I read the prompts for the October *Not Quite Write Prize*, something just clicked, and I saw how it might work well with the "head-hopping" anti-prompt. From there, Sienna's woeful tale began to take shape. Thankfully, her relationship with her father is not inspired by my own; however, I have definitely experienced the awful sticky-slap of thighs against the leather seat of a restaurant booth in my time!'

Ed's comments

Not feeling like you have any control over your life is a huge part of being a teenager. This story captures that feeling superbly through Sienna's tendency to make little wagers with herself, and we share her disappointment when her fears are proven true.

I love the way Sheridan has painted this picture of an absent, disinterested father and a daughter who deeply craves his affection, purely through subtext. There is no backstory or exposition here – it's a wonderful example of 'showing'.

Amanda's comments

This story opens with an elegant subterfuge – a subverting of the expectations set by just one line, 'Finish your essay by 8pm and tonight he'll call.'

We're not told in so many words that Sienna is a teenager, yet it's evident from the beginning, and so we naturally fall into the trap of assuming this line refers to a love interest.

Where some authors might be tempted to leave the rug-pull until the climax, Sheridan has wisely elected to reveal the truth right away. The result is that readers can enjoy that element of surprise while also fully investing in the emotion of the strained parent/child relationship.

This is one of those cases where I'd recommend ending a line or two sooner for greater impact, however Sheridan otherwise strikes the perfect balance between 'showing' and 'telling'. Readers are invited to connect the dots themselves, making for a deeply satisfying reading experience in this *other* relatable teen heartbreak story.

RIDE IT TO HEAVEN

W. J. Arthur

Caddy found it unsettling living in a street where the numbers started at thirteen. When the freeway went through, houses one to twelve disintegrated to make the great road of progress. Caddy's house, once in the centre, now hovered on the edge overlooking the incessant traffic.

Mrs Harborne, queen of the Anzac biscuits, died in the kitchen of number eight. Her house had been at the centre of the left lane, where the expansion joints are now. As Caddy lay in bed at night, she listened to the cars grinding over the metal. The rubber tyres became Charon's agents, chipping and carrying fragments of Mrs Harborne's soul over the bridge and across the river.

The nature strip was the boneyard of Mr Mackie's garden. It had been turned over when the house went down, but the banana passionfruit had self-seeded. After school, late on Wednesday afternoon, Caddy plucked some to make jam, stuffing them into the pockets of her hoodie. An honour drive of hippeastrums, defiant in red and pink, shamed the weeds and rubbish. Caddy looked in case something interesting had been tossed. Caddy had told her mother she was meeting Claire to do some photography on the bridge. Only, two elements weren't quite true, and Stew might take a photo, if she asked.

Stew was lounging against the barrier that saved the path from crumbling recklessly into the rushing cars. Traffic dashed at 100 kph this time of day, or faster. Caddy knew Stew had once clocked an easy 160, as she clinched onto his back. Stew leaned over the fence, tangled hair dancing in the car's currents. He flicked it back as Caddy approached, like a swimmer flicking off the wet. He was wearing the Green Day t-shirt that she had given him last Wednesday, the sleeves razor slit around his biceps, veins labouring beneath the tight sheath of his skin. Caddy's eyes traced the maze of his tattoo.

'Wake me when...' Stew sung.

'And a little package for the eye catcher,' Stew threw his keys, his lucky rabbit's foot slapping across Caddy's palm.

Leaning nearby, Stew's 1977 Triumph Bonneville in Jubilee red, white and blue, his open-faced helmet outstaring the ground. The hum of the freeway would mask the grunt and growl of the engine. If Caddy was quick, no one would call the cops. Caddy revved down the fence line, popping a wheelie until she reached the undercarriage footpath of the bridge. Caddy crouched low, lining up the path like a runway. She opened the throttle, quickly kicking through the gears, burning rubber.

Stew lay down, twisting his head sideways, hair splayed behind him. He watched Caddy as the shadows rose and retreated, the bike sometimes sparkling, sometimes dull and dark. He could feel the thrum of the motor reverberating through the concrete. It played in tune with the songs in his head, filling in the bass, whilst Stew played the air drums.

'You ride it to heaven girl,' he called.

'Ride it to heaven.'

About the author

Mid pandemic, W.J. Arthur's daughter proposed a challenge, to write a flash story every day. Arthur baulked, said it was impossible, but sat down to write. 1,404 flash fiction stories have been scrawled into life since, some average, some lousy and a few that are unforgettable.

Author's insights

'The long sightlines of Mt Henry Bridge and Kwinana Freeway offered inspiration for *Ride It To Heaven*. The freeway runs through the middle of Cranford Avenue in Brentwood and led to thoughts of the people that used to live there. I wondered if tiny fragments of our lives are treasured by the Earth. The prompt of incorporating a lie, made me think of the lies that we tell our parents. Caddy's lie of meeting with a boy instead of a friend, is a common one! My mum hates motorbikes, and learning to ride one was, out of necessity, quite a clandestine activity.'

Ed's comments

What makes this story special is what *doesn't* happen.

The unlucky number thirteen in the opening sentence, the brief vignettes about lives that were paved over and forgotten, the references to Hades – all these elements place a suggestion in the mind of the reader, evoking a nihilistic atmosphere that vibes perfectly with punk rock and motorbikes and living dangerously, foreshadowing a conclusion that is never spelled out.

I feel this open ending is more powerful, somehow serving to amplify the emptiness and futility embodied by these characters.

Amanda's comments

This piece was all about the vibes, and what better band to choose to represent Gen X nostalgia than Green Day?

W. J. drops us straight into this scene with a selection of (not sepia... but perhaps mid-noughties 'low saturation aesthetic') details, before delivering both an expert setup and payoff of the 'lie'.

I would have loved to have seen a full narrative arc play out against this beautiful backdrop, yet there's an implied end to this tale which carries the reader beyond the page. W. J. leaves us alone to reflect on what it means to grow old, what it means to die, and how only one of those things ever seems possible when we're young.

OCTOBER 2024 LONGLIST

The following list represents the remaining longlisted entries, in no particular order:

- **WILDCARD WINNER** – TABITHA PALMER WAS A PART OF ME FOR A SHORT TIME by Nikki Crutchley
- PRETENDER by A.C. Stewart
- A CONTINGENCY by Kelli Johnson
- THE FUTURE(S) SHE LEFT BEHIND by Tiffany Harris
- OH, TANNENBAUM! by Tabbie Hunt
- PERFECTION IN PAIN by Jordan Kemp
- LENS by Genevieve Flintham
- MIND THE GAP by Carla Connolly
- NEIGHBOURLY LOVE by Bob Topping
- AM FIBBING THINGS by Michelle Oliver
- THE EMBODIMENT OF DECEPTION by Paul Miller
- HeadHOPA by Anthea Jones
- BEAUTY SLEEP by Liv Hibbitt

- DEATH WAS WAITING by Chloee Thornhill
- **DISHONOURABLE MENTION** – TALKING HEADS: THE TALE OF JOHNSON & JOHNSON by Holly Sadowski
- GRANNY THEFT AUTO by Ruth Lord
- RISK AND ROMANCE FOR THE REGIONAL SALES MANAGER by Eloise Wajon
- FORGET JACOB DAVIS by Jaime Gill
- NURSE FRAN PROMISES SHE WILL NOT CHOP YOU INTO PIECES AND PUT YOU IN A PIE by Lorena Otes
- YOU'RE SOAKING IN IT. by Kerry Goldsworthy
- TO CARVE by Emma Graham
- LICE-FREE by Louise Walton
- DEAD GIRLS DON'T FEEL by M. Lea Gray
- WHAT CASSANDRA SAW by Elysia Rourke
- IN PIECES by Joanna Potenza
- WE'LL JUST CALL IT A DRIVE-BY by Roses Price
- I SEE YOU by Averil Robertson
- WHEN CRACKS BECOME CHASMS by Jaden Christopher
- NEVER TRUST AN ENGLISHMAN (ESPECIALLY NOT A REDHEAD) by Raphaela Power
- IT'S BLOODY MONKEY, NOT BLOODY MARY by N. M. Fadzli
- BOYS WILL BE BOYS by Lauren Dougherty
- SHUT THE F*** UP by Jo Skinner
- EVERY FIVE YEARS, I PULL A HAT TRICK by Chad Frame

- THE EXECUTIONER'S LAMENT by Greg Schmidt

The following story did not make the longlist but received a wildcard prize:

- **WILDCARD WINNER** – SHINING BLADE by Bia Ohtani

Note: Since 2024, each judge has awarded a wildcard prize to an entry which did not make the shortlist but which we otherwise felt deserved recognition. We sometimes award a cheeky 'Dishonourable mention' to a story which raises our eyebrows in a manner only known to its author.

Acknowledgements

Bravo to the authors whose prize-winning writing features in this book: Taurenelle, Tess Allen, Em Arata-Berkel, W. J. Arthur, Terra Babcock, R.C. Barajas, Sheridan Bell, Autumn Bettinger, Charles Byrne, George Faville, Eilish Forwells, Chad Frame, M. Lea Gray, Gwendaline Higgins, Tabbie Hunt, Sam James, Remy Joll, Dean Koorey, Roxanne Kubiak, Athena Law, J. Lewis-Edney, Kathy Prokhovnik, Laura J. Rayne, Emily Rinkema, Greg Schmidt, Sally Simon, Bob Topping, and Anne Wilkins. We bow to your talents, many and varied as they are, and look forward to watching you reach even higher heights in your personal writing journeys.

Thank you to our spouses, Sharon and Andy, and our daughters, Tara and Carissa, and Isla and Skye, for being our biggest cheerleaders and giving us the space to create and grow *Not Quite Write* and its component parts. We're eternally grateful for your patience and support for our silly nonsense.

A special thanks to Dean Koorey for your friendship and support (and for not suing us for stealing your idea).

ACKNOWLEDGEMENTS

Thanks also to the Coven: Jayne Rice (whose name also appears on page 60), Jess Popplewell, Jo Lyons, Julia Boggio, Farrah Riaz, and Cristal Phillips, for sprinkling your collective magic over Amanda's soul. We hope our readers will google you all immediately and buy all your books!

To our fellow Coasties, including the team behind Words on the Waves, the CoastWrite crew, and our beloved local booksellers, thanks for helping to spread the word about *Not Quite Write* and supporting our vibrant local writing community.

Thank you to Vanessa Browne for making us look good, and for making this book look even better. Your keen design eye and practised hand are without peer.

Finally, a huge thank you to ALL our *Not Quite Write Prize* entrants. Your passion for your writing is contagious, and we feel so honoured that you continue to trust us with your flash babies. From the shiniest of newbies, to the barnacle-encrusted stalwarts, we love you all.

Every entry, every social media share, and every word of encouragement and positivity you devote to helping *Not Quite Write* thrive is *so* appreciated. This competition is what YOU have made it, and we happen to think you've made something pretty special.

May the seeds of our first years together bear weird and wonderful, sometimes purple, often bitter, occasionally sweet, but perennially delectable fruit.

Inspired by these stories?

Why not enter the next round of the
Not Quite Write Prize for Flash Fiction?

notquitewriteprize.com

Praise for the Not Quite Write Prize

'This competition is great as a beginner writer because the podcasts give some insight into what worked and where writers could improve. Hopefully over time, that will all sink in.'
— *Heidi Couvee*

'This is my first attempt at flash fiction. I bought a ticket as a lawyer looking for creative ways to fall in love with writing again and am pressing submit as a new flash fiction enthusiast!'
— *Megwyn Mosenthal*

'The whole concept of the anti-prompt is so far up my alley, it's like crawling up the Skee-Ball ramp to drop one straight in the 1000-point bucket!'
— *Loquacious_Lamb*

'Every time I see an anti-prompt I think "What the hell have I gotten myself into?" But every time it somehow inspires me, and I don't think I ever have as much fun writing for comps as I do for yours.'
— *Greg Schmidt*

'The winning entries (and the short or longlisted entries) are some of the best competition entries I have ever read, so you've clearly found a way of inspiring writers to bring their A game.'
— *Lauren Dougherty*

Connect with us

The *Not Quite Write Podcast* is available on all major podcasting platforms. Search for us on your platform of choice or scan the QR code below.

notquitewrite.com

Connect with us on social media

 @notquitewrite.bsky.social

 @NQWpodcast

 @NotQuiteWritePodcast

 @NotQuiteWritePodcast

PO Box 9067
Wyoming NSW
AUSTRALIA 2250

contact@notquitewrite.com

We value your support

All books live or die on the recommendations of their readers. If you enjoyed this book, please spread the word!

You can support this book and its authors by:

- Buying a copy for yourself and/or loved ones
- Encouraging other people to buy a copy
- Rating and reviewing the book online
- Sharing a review on social media
- Talking about the book with other readers
- Liking and sharing *Not Quite Write* social media posts
- Performing ritualistic sacrifices in the book's honour

Thank you for all you do to support
the creative arts and artists.